house mother normal

B S Johnson

house mother normal
a geriatric comedy

Collins
St James's Place London 1971

for Glyn Tegai Hughes
and Gregynog

William Collins Sons & Co Ltd
London · Glasgow · Sydney · Auckland
Toronto · Johannesburg

First published 1971
© B S Johnson 1971
ISBN 0 00 221324 9

Set in Monotype Bembo
Made and Printed in Great Britain by
William Collins Sons & Co Ltd Glasgow

Friend (I may call you friend?), these are also
our friends. We no longer refer to them as
inmates, cases, patients, or even as clients.
These particular friends are also known as NERs,
since they have no effective relatives, are
orphans in reverse, it is often said.

You may if you wish join our Social Evening,
friend. You shall see into the minds of our
eight old friends, and you shall see into my
mind. You shall follow our Social Evening
through nine different minds!

Before entering each of our old friends' minds
you will find a few details which may be of
interest to you. A CQ count, for instance, is

given: that is, the total of correct answers
which were given in response to the ten classic
questions (Where are you now? What is this
place? What day is this? What month is it?
What year is it? How old are you? What is
your birthday? In what year were you born?
Who is on the throne now – king or queen?
Who was on the throne before?) for senile
dementia.

You find our friends dining, first, and later
singing, working, playing, travelling,
competing, discussing, and finally being
entertained.

age	74
marital status	widow
sight	60%
hearing	75%
touch	70%
taste	85%
smell	50%
movement	85%
CQ count	10
pathology	contractures; incipient hallux valgus; osteo-arthritis; suspected late paraphrenia; among others.

. . . not like this muck, they give us muck, here, I made him
a proper dinner, gave his belly a treat after all that Gas,
but he could hardly eat, the poor boy, what I put before him
was faggots in a lovely gravy, it was something special I
made, for him, just for him, then, not like this slimy brown
muck they slosh on everything here, can't think why they do
it, what the point is, not on my life, no.   And
I could see his eyes light up as he saw it, it was really
like being at home for him, that's when he realised it, for
the first time that first day, I think.
But then he couldn't eat it, the first mouthful and he was
sick, he had to rush out the yard to the carsey and I was
left – Now what's she done wrong?   Mrs Ridge
in trouble again, she asks for it, she must like the twitcher,
really.   I could hear him in there, standing
at the door as I was, looking at them faggots and the new peas

I'd shelled that morning, and thniking of the butter I'd
mashed his taties with and how little Ronnie had had to go
without for a week, though I gave him his Dad's later, he
did enjoy it, that day, for his tea.

And when he came in from the yard you could
tell he was that ill, by his colour, and he asked me to come
up and lie on the bed with him, and I did, though it was just
after midday, and he just sort of   lie
there, with his eyes shut and his face all
                                             tight,
without bothering to turn down the counterpane to rest his
head on the pillow, and it was greasy with brilliantine or
something suchlike, but I couldn't say anything could I?

Not that he touched me, he lie there with his hands crossed
across his belly, like he was dead already, not touching me,
just wanting me near him, he said, to feel I was there, and
I don't think he could have done anything with me anyway,
then, it was   months before he was a real husband
to me again, ah.

                                                              Clear
up, clear up, it's all on the hurryup in this place.
                                        Now what's she
saying, how can you be quiet about clearing up knives and
forks, how can anyone? Though these cardboard plates
can't make any noise, because if – *Here, Ivy, no, I
haven't finished yet!* Last scrapings of this muck,
muck they give us here, but I'm hungry, there's nothing
else, nothing.   There. I'll walk, at least I can still
walk, though that means she makes me do the running about.
I have to clear up and wait on the others, these bent forks
and knives, the knives not sharp at all, down here, I'm
not washing up today, the sitters can at least do that,
sitters can – Now Mrs Bowen's knocked her plate down,
now she'll cop it.   Yes.

                                               Her and that
dog, shouldn't be surprised if House Mothers aren't
really supposed to keep pets, could write to them about
it, her and that bloody great dog
                        Get on with it, help Ivy, get on.
                                        She won't get
it done sooner by shouting at me, I go as fast as I
can, yes I do, can't go any faster.

                   Nearly done.

There, at last that's done, sit down again, next to
Charlie, later I'll get round him for a cigarette, I
know he's got some.   Oh, not
that song again.   What good does it
do?

                              Better sing, though, don't
want to cross her again, no.

> *The joys of life continue strong*
> *Throughout old age, however long:*
> *If only we can cheerful stay*
> *And brightly welcome every day.*
> *Not what we've been, not what we'll be,*
> *What matters most is that we're free:*
> *The joys of life continue strong*
> *Throughout old age, however long.*

> *The most important thing to do*
> *Is stay alive and see it through:*
> *No matter if the future's dim,*
> *Just keep straight on and trust in Him:*
> *For He knows best, and brings good cheer,*
> *Oh, lucky us, that we are here!*
> *The most important thing to do*
> *Is stay alive and see it through!*

                              Well, I suppose it
pleases Her, at any rate.

Listen to
her now, work, work, I've known nothing else all
my life, who does she think she's taking in?
Good deed indeed, she must make something out
of all this, though it's not sweated labour by
any manner of means, I will say that for her, it's
not arduous, and she can't get much for these
Christmas crackers they make, wonder who does
the fillings, the mottoes, we used to enjoy
crackers that Christmas before he went, there was
an old-fashioned Christmas if you like, it snowed
that year it did, very unusual for London to snow
on Christmas Day, don't remember any other years
it happened, in fact, and how it changed the look
of everything, people started acting differently,
too, people you knew only to nod at suddenly
joined in snowballing in the street outside as
though you'd all been kids together, had grown up
in the same street.   And we had some money for
a change, had a bird instead of a joint, a capon,
the baby had some giblet gravy with roast potato
mashed up in it, very nourishing for him it was.

Knowing he was for the Front made him
depressed, then suddenly he'd be so cheerful, such good
company, he made it a wonderful Christmas for all of
us, him and his brother, they did a sort of act for
us, Jim got up as a woman, makeup and all, we ached
from laughing, they were so comical, the pair of them,
ached from eating too much, as well, I never – *Me?*
Me and Charlie?   Trusties, she talks to us

as though we were doing bird, indeed, one of these
days I'll show her how trusty I am!
What's Charlie got in them bottles, then?
Looks like gin, smells like spirits, too – she
must be at it again, the crafty old chiseller!
Still, what's it got to do with me?
Glad I haven't got the job, anyway, never could
stomach the smell of spirits, I told him that before
we were married, stick to your pint, I said,
don't you come home here reeking to high heaven of
spirits, I won't have it in my home.

Yes?

Little bottles, what are they?
Soak the labels off, I bet.   Use the bowl from
the sink, I'll stand them in that, in water, would
some soap help? *Do you want me to keep the labels?*

My nails are broken, have been for years,
but give the bottles a good old soak and they'll come
off. *Shall I use a knife?*

Good, this is an
easy job, I can get on with that, it helps to pass the
time, I don't mind, get the bowl, fill it with water.

What's in these little bottles? Chloro-benzo. . . .
Can't read it properly, whatever it is. No matter, none
of my business anyway. *Charlie, have you got a fag?*

Mean old sod. And
I know he smokes. Like my Ronnie, always telling
lies, I'd catch him with the fag in his hand
and he'd put it behind his back and drop it and
breathe out the smoke all over the kitchen and
swear he wasn't smoking at all.
And he married a like one, his kind, oh I hated
that creature, bad as my Ronnie was he didn't
deserve her, no, never.   Lie, she would
lie her way black and blue out of anything, you
could catch her out any number of times and she
would still deny it. I gave up in the end, you
just couldn't rely on anything she said, anything
at all, anything even as simple as just meeting
you for shopping, she'd lie about who she'd just
seen and what she'd just bought and how much
money she'd won on the bleeding dogs. I'd no time
for her, it must be twenty years since I saw her,
fifteen since I last saw my Ronnie, too. He came
into the pub we had in Strutton Ground then, I
was so surprised to see him walk in, he had a
Guinness and no more than a dozen words to say to
me, a dozen words, and most of them he could
hardly get out, he was that ashamed, I think,
ashamed of not going to see his old Mum for all
that length of time, months it was, perhaps a year.
Not like Laura's son, twice a week he used to
visit her regularly, once for a cup of coffee at
lunchtime early in the week, and later – There,
that's enough soaking, let's see if these little

labels will come off now.
No, tough little customers they are, it's not
waterproof paper, is it, can't be?

Perhaps it would help if I scratched them a bit,
to let the water soak in better. A fork would
do it.

Yes, that's easier, let's try doing that
to all of them.

I wonder if
Ronnie knows I'm here?   Not that he'd want
to visit me, no one gets any visitors here,
anyway, but I'd like to see him just the once more
before I pass over, just the once.   He
wouldn't have to see me if he didn't want to, no,
as long as I could see him, out of a window,
perhaps, going along the road, just the once.

As long as she wasn't
with him, the barren sow, she could never give him
any kids, and I know he always wanted kids, my
Ronnie, he was ever so good with them, look how
he used to go and play football with them until
he was quite a grown man, used to run a team for
them as well, he used to get me to wash the team
shirts each week in the winter, it was a trial
getting them dry, it was, she wouldn't wash them,
I doubt if she washed Ronnie's own things properly,

let alone the team's, she was that lazy, Doris
was her name, yes, Doris, I wouldn't want to see
her again, no, just my Ronnie, once.

        Does he think I'm dead? How could
he know I'm here? Could I find him?   How?
Could ask House Mother.   She'd laugh at the
idea, brush it aside, take no notice, I'm
afraid   of her

            Not her!
Now let's see if they'll come off   Yes,
nearly there, if I have a good scrape at this one
then by the time it's off the others will be even
more soaked, all ready.

        What does she want with them?
Yellowy sort of stuff inside, yellowy, runny.
Nasty-looking stuff.

In summer there everyone seemed to take life
easily, so easily, it was as though there were
no pain, no work either, everyone had time to
just walk about, go swimming, sunbathing, get
up boat races, and go dancing. They danced a
new dance called the gavotte, or it was new to
me, anyway, being a foreigner. And they danced
in the streets, too, that was new, the streets
lit by paper lanterns in their fashion. And the
sun so hot at midday that the market-women
put up their red umbrellas for shade, and the
men went into these sort of cellar pubs that sold
wine, I never went into one, could only see down

into them that they were cool and shaded, and there
was a lot of laughing and the tables had zinc
tops and so did the bar, a long bar, the bottles
kept in holes, no labels, I was so thirsty I
went to a café down on the promenade with the
children, little Ronnie was all right but that Clarissa
was a little bastard to me, she knew she could
play me up with safety and she took advantage
of it.   I could have been so happy
there, there was so much sun and the life was easy
apart from Clarissa, and she was my job, to
let her parents have some time free, free of her,
that is, for she was a little bastard to them
as well as to me.   I wonder what she
could have become, she was already an Hon., I
think, Clarissa, and it was doing little Ronnie
so much good, the sea air and three good meals a
day, the food was good in that hotel, even for
those in service, and it seemed as though it
would go on for ever, the summer, the sun, and
for the first time since the War I really felt
that things were getting back to normal, though
all the ones who could remember better than I
could were saying that things would never be the
same, never could be, after the War, which I could
understand in the case of someone like myself,
who'd lost their husband because of the War, but
not those who'd not lost their nearest and dearest
in it.   And it was there I
think I first got over Jim's death, not got over

it, exactly, but accepted my lot, that I was a
young widow with a young kid, like lots of
others, that this was what my life was, that
this was what I was. In that seaside town in
France, France where Jim had got Gassed, though
not the same place, of course, and I think
Clarissa's father may have had something to do
with it, it was the first time I had seen a
man's parts when he tried to get me down on
my hotel bed, since Jim's, that is, and I think
that must have made me realise there were other
men in the world, seems silly now, though at the
time it was a frightening thing to happen,
perhaps if he'd asked me, or gone about it in a
different way, I'd have let him, though I knew
it was wrong and I respected his wife, I might
even have enjoyed it, it was two years since Jim
had gone, but he was so rough and arrogant with
it, he seemed to think because I was a servant he
could order me about in anything, order me to do
that like he could order me to clean his shoes,
which I didn't like, the brazenness of it, just
came up to me while I was at my dressing-table,
unbuttoned already he was, and seized my hand and
made me hold his part, and when I drew back,
naturally, he got rough and threw me on the bed and
would have had his way with me had I not yelled and
screamed fit to make the whole hotel hear. And
so he got up and buttoned himself up with his back
to me, swearing all the time vilely at me, and

little Ronnie woken up by all this noise, standing
up in his cot and wondering what was happening to
his Mum. And of course I didn't last long after
that, he couldn't look at me after that.
Clear up now. Nearly finished. Just scrape off
these last two.

There. Now give them all a wipe.

And put them all back in their nice little cardboard
sockets.   One   two   three   four
five   six   seven   eight
one   two   three   four   five
six   seven   sixteen
one two   three   four   five   six
seven   twenty-four
one   two   three   four   five
six   seven   eight
one   two   three   four   five
six   seven   sixteen
one   two   three   four   five
six   seven   forty-eight, two cases of
twenty-four is what I started with. The satisfaction
of finishing. A job well done.

Here, Missus, I've finished.

How nice to be thanked.   The warmth.
                          Very pleased indeed, she said.

That pleases me. A job well done. And the time
passed, too. Now what's she want?

Pass the Parcel? We used
to play that, didn't we? Don't want to
play much now. Why does she give us games?
I just want to sit quietly after working so much.
But I suppose I'd better be sociable.

Me to start?
Off. Pass it to Charlie. What is it? Brown
paper, soft.

It's stopped at Mrs Ridge first, but she won't be
able to open it all in time.

Oh! It's stopped at me!
Open, open, get the paper off, I won't be the
winner, there, it's started again.
Stink. . . . What is it!

Ron's got it, he'll get it open. *What is it, Ron?*
How disgusting!
Why does she do a thing like that?
Glad I didn't win, glad I
didn't win!

It was the third husband I'd buried, I was getting
used to it. All the market crowd in Strutton
Ground chipped in and gave him a great send-off,
he was a popular landlord. Flowers, I never saw
so many flowers. And the customers, too, bought
the odd one for Fred, they did.   But
it didn't worry me too much. The brewers let me
take on the licence, and within weeks it was just
the same, as though he'd never existed. That
pub used to have a sort of life of its own, then.
And during the war of course you didn't have to
sell beer, it sold itself, it was getting hold
of enough of it that was the difficulty. Oh yes.
And crisps. There was only one place you could
generally get crisps, then, and that was up on
the North Circular Road. Many's the time I've
caught a trolleybus up the Edgware Road to Staples
Corner and come – Exercise?   Haven't we
had enough?   Oh well, up we get. It's not
for long. She thinks it does us good, perhaps it
does. It doesn't kill me, anyway.
              I'll push that George Hedbury
round. Not much company, but there you are.

Off we go! *George, can you hear me?* Deaf as a
post, deaf as a post, daft as a doughnut.
One two three four! Round and round, round and
round!

And so it goes on.   That Laura

was a great one for her Guinness. Sometimes I've
seen her knock back thirty in an evening. But
she was a quiet drinker. You'd never know
she'd had too many till she fell down when she
tried to get up. This bloody pushchair needs
oiling or something. But she was a good friend
to me, we had many a good time together. She
pulled me out of many a dark time. Like when
Ronnie married that Doris. And after the cat
got run over, Maisie.

We kids used to run about in felt
slippers then, they were the cheapest, a cut above
the barefoot kids. It was our way of

Tired of pushing. But still carry on. Slog, slog.

They were the good old days, it's true.

And where were we when we were wanted? Oh, we
were there all right, slapping the sandbags on
the incendiaries, ducking down the shelters when
the HE started. All that sort of thing.
That's enough. I can't push any more. I'm going
to stop whether she likes it or not, going to stop.

                    A sit at last,
rest my legs.

Sport! She certainly keeps us on the go.

Tourney. That means me pushing someone, I suppose.
                    Up again, Sarah, you can do it.
Lean on George's bathchair till I have to move, take
the nearest corner, Charlie'll have to go further
with Mrs Bowen.
George doesn't seem too well. Prop the mop under
his arm, keep it steady.

                                    Ready!
                                        Go!
            Trundle, trundle, not as young as I used to
be, get up speed.   There!
            Silly old fool let the mop drop and caught
hers in the chops!
                        Not so fast this time.
Keep up the mop now, George!
                    There, that must have hurt him.
You all right?   Seems all right.
                                    I should think it
is the last time!

                        Ooooh! That surely
hurt him. But he says nothing, George, just takes it.

Wheel him over to his place and sit down again.
                                My legs are getting
worse, I'm sure they swell up with all this standing.
It's like a dull ache.

Poor old thing.   Let her talk
away, I'm not interested, it's a rest for me. And
my poor legs.
On his back for months, my Jim, going slowly, you
couldn't see it day by day, but suddenly I'd
realise that compared with a month or so before he was
definitely down. And he found it difficult to talk,
more and more. For days I knew he was trying to
bring himself to say something, and then it all
came out. He'd been with some girl in France, they
all did, he said, went to some brothel, and he was
so guilty about it, as though it were some great
crime he'd committed. Perhaps it was to him, then.
But to me it didn't matter, because I could see
he was dying, everybody could, nothing seemed to
matter but that fact and that I had to make the
most of what there was, nothing in the past
mattered, neither the good things nor the others, his
guilt was of no interest to me, or the girl, I
just forgave him as he seemed to want me to, and
it did relieve his mind, you could see that, he
just sank back, and very quickly fell asleep.
                                He kept a spit-bowl
by his bed, that was the worst part, emptying that,
the yellowy green stuff and the blood, he couldn't

get out to the carsey, either, but somehow
emptying his spit-bowl was worse, like throwing
away bits that were him.

                                   I tell them
my troubles, they tell me theirs.

We had a good feed at a chip place, before he
went off to his football. I went round the
shops, all excited inside all the afternoon.
Perhaps it was expecting what – Laugh? *Ha ha
ha*, *ho ho ho*.
I wish I'd been kind to old people then, now I
know how it is. It's always the same, you can
never know until you actually are. And then
it's too late. You realise which are the important
things only when it's too late, that's the
trouble.
                   However much he made it was
always too little, I always had to watch every
penny so carefully. In the butchers I had to take
what he'd give me cheap, and his dirt and insolence.
No one has ever treated me like a queen.
You'd think every girl would be treated like a queen
by someone at some time in her life, wouldn't you?
But not me. Perhaps I never deserved it, perhaps

I never treated any man like a king.

          Now what's she rucking Ivy for?

                    Oh, she's going through that again,
is she? She don't half fancy herself! Well, I
don't, and it's filthy so I shan't watch though
she may think I am.   My idea of a holiday
was never the sea, anyway. On those pub outings
they never looked at the sea in any case, all
they were interested in looking at was the insides
of the pubs along the front at Southend, one after
the other. They went into the first next to the
coach park and so it went on, all along the front.
They'd give the stakeholder half a quid each
and he'd buy the drinks as long as the money lasted.
                         You could get big fat
oysters on one stall, only time I ever enjoyed them
was down there. My dad would never eat shellfish
but once a year down at Southend, said they were
never fresh anywhere else. Cockles I'd have, too,
and those little brown English shrimps, very tasty,
but whelks I never could stand, far too gristly
and tough.   The Kursaal bored me, but
all the men used to love it when the pubs were
shut – What a disgusting spectacle!   Why
does she do it?
                         Disgusting!

Ugh! Never did like it, had to pretend, all my life pretended to like it.

Listen to her!

No, doesn't matter

age	78
marital status	separated
sight	50%
hearing	80%
touch	80%
taste	95%
smell	30%
movement	85%
CQ count	10
pathology	contractures; bronchitis; incipient leather bottle stomach; hypertension; among others.

I have always liked a lamb chop.   Even in the last
days I managed to have a lamb chop once a week.   Welsh
lamb I found the best, though New Zealand is a close second
in my opinion.   Even Betty knew that to please me she
had only to give me a lamb chop.   Here the lamb chops
are mutton, I am certain.   They are too big for any
lamb.   Where does a lamb end and a sheep begin?
                                   I used to see them in the
fields.   I know these are mutton. Sometimes they are
tough.   They are not always tough, though. They are
always stronger in taste than lamb.   Lamb has a delicate
flavour. The best lamb, that is, of course.   Mutton
tastes – again, every mealtime, that Mrs Ridge.
                           Strong mutton is not
without its own special attraction, of course.   Perhaps
if I had not tasted lamb first I would have come to like mutton

more.   One day she will go too far and someone will
report her to the authorities.   Whoever the authorities
are.

Yes, perhaps I would now like mutton if I had tasted it
before lamb.   It is an accident.
Perhaps.   I can
understand that they have mutton here rather than lamb.
                        It is for cheapness.
I am fortunate to be here.   And mutton keeps me
going as well as ever lamb would.   That is
their point of view, I am sure.   Mutton has
enough of the taste of lamb to make me remember.

                        I do not miss lamb now.
                I do not miss anything now. There is
no point.

It is hard.   Harder where there's none,
as my old Mum used to say.
                        Harder where there's none.

I still enjoy my food.   I am lucky in that.
                        Some of these poor old souls here
do not even have that pleasure.

                And it is a pleasure to me.
                        I am lucky to be here.

Some would revolt at some of the things that woman
says.   I do myself.   But I keep my feelings
to myself.   It would not do to be seen to
revolt, I am in some ways revolting in myself.
            Sometimes I have to be changed, like a baby.
Is that revolting?   I finish my food cleanly,
a clean plate.   I place my knife and my
fork as I was taught to do as a child.   It is
easy for Sarah to pick them up with one movement.
I am a tidy man.   I have been called fastidious
by some.   Betty had another word for it,
                what was it? She hated my tidiness,
anyway. As one gets older it becomes more and more
difficult to control the ordin. . . . Now there'll
be a fuss. Just over dropping a plate.
            I noticed it first with spitting, for sometimes
I would spit when speaking. And not always when
I spoke with some vehemence, either.   Sometimes
I would spit without any warning.   Even without
there seeming to be any reason for it, too. I found
it disturbing, but it was as nothing compared with
what there was to come   I found myself
not wanting to . . .   not minding about spitting
when I spoke.   Is that
worse?   Sometimes I cannot worry about things
like that.   Yet there is always a worse.
I have only to look at some of these poor old things
here to know that.   I am not as bad
as some.   I am lucky in that.   I am always
more than ready to count my   blessings.

Life has taught me at least that.   I can at least say that I was not a slow learner as regards life's lessons.   As though anyone should ask – the Song. She wants us to sing, as usual. Well, singing is something I have always enjoyed. The music teacher asked me to sing in his choir, outside school. It was a church choir, in Haggerston. Not because of your voice, he said, but because of your ear. You have perfect pitch. It was something unusual about me others did not have.

The joys of life continue strong
Throughout old age, however long:
If only we can cheerful stay
And brightly welcome every day.
Not what we've been, not what we'll be,
What matters most is that we're free:
The joys of life continue strong
Throughout old age, however long.

The most important thing to do
Is stay alive and see it through:
No matter if the future's dim,
Just keep straight on and trust in Him:
For He knows best, and brings good cheer,
Oh, lucky us, that we are here!
The most important thing to do
Is stay alive and see it through!

                There was word amongst the boys that the music teacher was bent.   I never saw it myself.

Work? I'm retired,
I'm not here to work. Though what she
calls work is not what I would call work.

Fancy goods, fancy goods. She
thinks she's a pretty piece of Fancy goods!

Not my fault. I wasn't on Fancy
goods last time. That is a relief,
she can't blame me.
Relief.

Crêpe paper.
Crêpe? Crêpe, crêpe, what a word.
crêpe.

Crêpe.

Reason, I have always believed in reason. It
was only necessary to be reasonable to be saved.
But I have found many in my time
who have disagreed. It is
not important.

Ah, now what does she want me to do tonight?

Good that she relies on me, that she –
                 Pour about a quarter
into   these empty ones. How many
empty ones?   Several dozen. I see. What is
it in the bottles? No colour, like water. Even
when I open one I shall not necessarily know, since
my sense of smell is not – *Yes, I understand.* What's
it say on the labels?   BOAKA, BOAKA? Can't
understand that.
*No, I'll be very careful. I haven't let you down
yet, have I?*

      What's she going to give her to do?
Nosy. I should mind my own.   But she's
got bottles, too. Little bottles. They look snug
in their little cardboard compartments.
                    Messy. Glad I
haven't got a messy job.   She'll get all
messy doing that.   I shan't, just pouring.
I am a very careful pourer. That's why she
chooses me to do these special jobs.
Let us apply reason to this job. If I stand a line
of empty bottles up, with a line of full ones in
front of them. . . .   No, that wouldn't be
very efficient because I'd have to keep moving the
full ones anyway. Try again.
                If I fill the empty
ones a quarter-full with water, then I can pour
from three full ones to top it up. Yes. A dozen
at a time might be a suitable number to – Now

what's she want?   *No, Sarah, you know*
I haven't got a cigarette. Disturbing my
reasonable deliberations. Now then, let's try
filling a dozen empties a quarter-full with
water. When Sarah's finished at the sink.

Line the dozen up, and a dozen full in front, and
pour . . .   yes, a quarter each from three full
ones   and I've got a finished
one. But what does she want me to do about
the corks?   Does she want them corked? I haven't
enough corks to go round. Still, that's her problem.
She'd have told me if she'd wanted them corked. Now
another – no, wait a minute, mate, here's a better
way. If you pour water from three of the quarter-
filled empties into the three you quarter-emptied –
better still if you'd filled the empties right to
the top with water, but for one or two. Then you
could have. . . .   That's it, Charlie
boy, you've got a scheme now. It's all sewn up. Off
you go, back to the sink for more water.

Easy now. Filling and pouring.   Straightforward
for a careful person with at least some intelligence.
Like I am.   Straightforward. I can do it
without thinking after a short while. Even might get
to like it without too much trouble. Same as during

the War. Soon learnt to get on with it and
like it. Got out of being sent on one draft
because I was the aerodrome pianist, but couldn't
dodge the second one. The first one I actually
left Dover aerodrome and was at Walmer
preparatory for leaving for the Front. But the
officer at Dover rang up and said Have you got
Edwards there? And they said Yes, he's doing a
good job clerking. Well, he'll do a better job
playing the Joanna here, he said, send him back
at once. So I went back in a staff car. Just
as we arrived there was a general alert throughout
the whole Dover Patrol and everyone leapt about.
Either bombs or shells were exploding as we drove
across the approach roads. But no one got hurt.
It was remarkable like that. So I was back to
organising socials and dances and concerts. By
the end of '15 I was pianist and leader of an eight-
piece. The personnel changed, of course, as people
got drafted, but somehow our officer always avoided
sending me until the autumn of '16, when I had to go.
But the year and a bit I was there stood me in good
stead. If it hadn't been for the experience I got
then I don't think I would have become a pro after
the War. I found I was better at it than I thought
I was. And I was making a tidy bit on the side
from it, too. It was then I first realised that
there was money to be made in this music game, far
more money than in the clerking I had been doing
up to then in the Civil Service. My disability

pension wasn't much when I came out, but it was just
enough to keep me going until I got myself a job
playing in a cinema. A white sheet hanging up by its
four corners in a church hall in Kingsland High
Street. They didn't listen to what the pianist was
playing. They only heard you if what you played
didn't fit in with what was on the screen. I'd
never really been to the pictures until then. But
I soon enough picked up what was wanted. You had
to keep on playing no matter what. They noticed if
you stopped. Sometimes they would applaud. Since
I was the only one live who had anything to do with
it it used to amuse me. I would take a bow as if
I were Paderewski or someone like that. Sometimes
we had a drumkit and other sound effects. The new
films came in twice a week or sometimes oftener.
I did not usually get any chance to see them before
the first house. That was the worst house, too.
They booed and yelled as if they were at a prize
fight.   There. That's the first
dozen. Put them into their crate.
Suppose this must be liquor of some sort. My sense
of smell is nearly gone. I'd be lost in a fire. But
don't ask questions. That's why she puts her trust
in me. But can't help wondering to myself what it
is. Or where it's going. Perhaps it's going to one
of those clubs like I used to play in in the twenties.
Before the rift came with Betty. Like the famous or
notorious Mrs Marshall's All-Up Club in Frith Street.
All that dust-up in the papers over bribing a

police sergeant. They were all taking. It was not
only the sergeant. Mrs Marshall was just the type
who would buy watered whisky. Or stolen whisky. Then
she'd water it down herself. The customers were
always complaining about the drink. She was very firm
with them. She tried to run it as she would her own
home, silly as it may sound. That's what she said
to anyone who complained, however. One night the
place would be full of gangsters, and the next you
might even have royalty there. There was no telling.
And it was all Mrs Marshall's doing. She was that
kind of powerful   phooooooor . . . rt! that's better,
woman. No man could dominate her, no indeed. She
had her man, or rather men, of course. But one at a
time. I've seen that woman set a man quivering with
fear just with one look. That was enough. And he
went sneaking out of the door just like a whipped cur.
Yet she was kind enough when she wanted to be. She
was very kind to me in her way. She could see that
I was dotty about Betty at the time, so there was
never any question of my wanting to make advances to
her. So really right from the start it was purely
a business association. I could get her the quality
players she needed for a place like that. And at
the same time those boys were the souls of discretion
itself about who they might see there and what they
might see going on. And they needed to be.
To people like us she was a good payer, too. I had
no gripes. The only bandsman I really had trouble
with was Ronnie Palmer. Later he made a name for

himself, of a sort, on the wireless as a kind of
poor man's Harry Lauder. But then he was violin
doubling saxes for me at Mrs M's All-Up. Ronnie
was ill-bred anyway, and a bit too fond of the
ladies with it. So fond that he was arranging for
them to be available during band breaks and other
odd times. Mrs M. wasn't keen on this on her own
premises, especially when it involved several of
the girls she had as cashiers and so on. But
when she spoke sharply to him about it, he answered
back. But he only just began to say something
that I think meant he could blackmail her in some
way and she was on him. First of all she thumped
him, and how he knew he'd been thumped, too, then
before he could think what he was doing she'd got
an arm-hold on him and had bounced him all the way
to the back, where one of the kitchen porters took
over and bounced him out to the dustbins. We
had to get through that night without Ronnie. It
was too late to find anyone to dep. for him.
Perhaps it did him a good turn in the end. Next
I heard of him he was in the BBC's own dance
orchestra. Perhaps I should have tried to get
into the wireless end of the business then. If I
had had foresight. Then I'd have had all the trouble
and all the jealousies and a hundred to one I
wouldn't have lived to be the age I am now. I should
count my blessings. Where's Ronnie Palmer now?
Dead, I should think. And he was younger than me.
It would have pleased Betty though if I'd managed to

be on the wireless. She was a great one for
that kind of thing.　　　　　Finished them
just in time. All full. What about corks?

　　　　　　　　　Here she comes,
down. *What shall I do for corks for these, Miss?*

Yes, I put those back afterwards.

Right, Miss. I don't know about the lifting, Miss. . . .
She's not listening. After that so-and-so dog again,
hairs everywhere.
Cork up. Dozens here in this box. Where does she
get them?　　　　　Anyway, they fit, won't
take me long to finish this lot.

Fingers can do this easily enough. I still hear
pieces in my head, but I couldn't play them even
if she had a piano here.

　　　　　　Now she's having another go at
that poor old soul. Though she asks for it in some
ways, I'll admit.　　　　　There, that's
the lot. I won't lift them. I don't want to strain
my gut.
　　　　　　Praising that Sarah. I've done
just as well. *What about me?*

I should think so, too.

Now what is it she's going to get us up to?
Pass the Parcel. Pass the
Parcel. This is stupid. Who wants to play silly
games? But we all do. We all do as she says.
Always.   Stupid.

A lovely surprise. I can imagine.

For me?

Pass it on to Ivy.

Mrs Ridge   She's about
half opened it.

Coming to me   Now to me, it'll come to
me!   Not quite.
Sarah's got it. Not fair. Injustice again.
What's in it? There, she didn't have time to win.
Hold on in case it stops now.   Have
to pass it now.   Not fair.

Pass it on!

Ron. It's that Ron.
Ha ha ha ha ha ha ha ha ha ha
ha ha!   *Ha ha* I shall
choke! That serves him right! *Ha ha ha ha ha ha*
ha ha ha ha ha!   Oh dearie me, dearie me, *ha ha!*

Ha ha!   ha ha ha ha ha!

It's like in Verdun. That fellow who couldn't
speak Flemish, or French was it. He was having
dinner in some café. Lamb he thought it was. He
enjoyed it so much that he tried to say how pleased
he was to the proprietor by pointing at his plate
and going "baa-baa" with a pleasant, questioning
look. But the proprietor grinned, shook his head and
said "bow-wow!" It's just a story. It must be just
a story. Though anything could happen out there.
You could believe anything. And though they said
that cities were bad places to live, they certainly
produced the best fighters. That's what I found.
Paris, too. They had more guts. They had had to
fight all their lives. It was natural. We were
attached to the French there. Rum once a week if
you were lucky. Once it didn't get through. Next
day we found the rum rationer dead on the road, not
dead drunk as we thought at first – Travel? I've
done enough of that in my time, if you don't mind.
Her name for the exercise session.   Stretch my
legs. Could do with a stretch.
Ah.   *Mrs Bowen,*
shall I give you a turn round?

> *Yes, I feel fine. Just for a few minutes,*
> *eh? I'm sure she won't want to keep us at it too*
> *long tonight, eh, Mrs Bowen?*

It was the guns all night. Then over the top at
dawn. Why wasn't I killed like most of my mates?
It's a mystery. No one can know. I had the new
shrapnel helmet on for the first time anything
came near my head. Left me a little concussed,
that's all. Another time a Jerry got me across
it with the butt end of his rifle. But it didn't
affect me and I got him with my bayonet while he
was recovering from the swing. I'd got used to the
noises people made, by then. It was him or me, I
knew that.

I saw a Jerry using
his spiked helmet as a weapon. Hand-to-hand it
was by then, in some attacks. When there were
gas shells about you tried to get a Jerry's gas-
mask off.
Some of those old songs still turn me over.

March, march, left, right, left right, left right,
left! *Don't feel nervous on the corners, do you
Mrs B?*   *Good.*

I also saw gunners chained to their pieces to
stop them running for it. I saw officers urge
their men on from the rear with revolvers in their
hands. A man shot dead for answering back one of
the officers. Two weeks before the Armistice my
own cousin told me his officer had it in for him
and would certainly see to it that he got sent up

to the Front right to the last. He was blown
up with his gun. Serving his gun bravely to the
end, that so and so wrote to my poor Auntie.
Sent her the bits and pieces left, his brass
numbers all buckled, a tiny wineglass not broken, a
present for his daughter, she decided. And there
amongst the – Tourney? Right.
Right, Mrs Bowen,
sport now. You won the tourney last time, didn't
you? You can do it again!
Thanks, Ivy.
Take the soggy mop.

Oh, this is a right
lark!

Off! Thunder
off! Better start than Sarah,
faster top speed, better knight, harder *IMPACT!*
Very good, Mrs Bowen, right in the face!
Round we go. And back again,
we'll have another go.
BOMPF!
Right in the shoulder, Mrs Bowen!
And again. We'll be the win-
ners, two-nil up.

Tiring. *THUMP! Well done us, Mrs*
Bowen, we deserve a rest, eh?
Well done!

I don't want to listen to
all that rubbish again. Who does she think I am?
Bill and Glory asked
me to come and play in their pub in the city. I'd
never played in pubs before that. Because of my
disability I could not be called up. I was too
old anyway. But I had to go into industry, everybody had to do that. I had nothing to do at night
times only go down the shelter or hide out in the
suburbs. So I was quite pleased to have something
to do. Shortly afterwards America came into the
war, and they used to pour out of Liverpool Street
station straight into this pub right opposite.
Somehow it seemed that the way I played was just
their handwriting. The word got around the
aerodromes in East Anglia and the pub did a roaring
trade. They would come in there with their five
days' leave and lots of lovely money in their
pockets and say 'Sing us the songs the old man sang in
the last war.' They used to have a good time, I
was better off than I had been for a long time.

Nothing comes from nothing, I was
taught. But what about plants? The space occupied
by the growth must have left a space behind?
A field of wheat must surely have sunk by the volume

of the growth? If not, why not? These questions
should be answered.   House
mother up on the dais again. Surely she's not going to tell us all those jokes again?
                    Yes, she is.

                         Groan, not laugh.
Heard it before. Shan't listen.   The
places I can't reach. They must be getting very
dirty. Can't scratch them properly, either. They
might be festering. They get wet when I bath, but
not washed. I am not allowed to be as fastidious
as I was. Or rather I am unable – Laugh! On the
word Laugh! you will laugh as ordered. *Ha Ha Ha!*

                         I went too far after the
rift with Betty. I just walked out on a job the
day after, and walked and walked all over, not knowing – *Groan, groan!*   I didn't
care whether I lived or died. As it happened, I
lived. I don't know how, at first. We had met too
many well-to-do people on our tours, and the girl
became dissatisfied. I can understand that now. At
the time it seemed bound to happen and very painful.
I went hungry once or twice, but soon found how to
ask for things with a fair chance of – *HA HA HA!*
                    I also offered to do

little jobs to help people out in return for the
odd meal or place to sleep for the night, and I
usually managed – Now what's Ivy done?
                                Poor old girl. Just reading
her book quietly.

                                                Who
wants to see hers? I've seen plenty of them in my
time, enough to last me a lifetime, thank you very
much. As for that great hairy dog. . . .
                                One day I thought to myself
I can do better than this, so I went into a shop
and bought myself a penny whistle. It was a brass
one because they told me a tin one was illegal.
And as the fingering was the same as on the little
fife I learnt to play at school, it was quite easy
for me to pick out a few tunes. So from then on I
used to go drifting about all over the country playing
my little whistle and picking up enough coppers
to keep me going. But there were times when it was
hard. People wouldn't give money to a young chap
of thirty-three or four or five who looked so hale
and hearty. They thought I should get a job, not
go begging around the streets with a penny whistle.
Some of them told me so, too. One man went so far
as to knock me down in the gutter, saying he hadn't
fought the war for beggars, or something like that.
So I showed him my disability, and then he – Oh,
filth, utter filth! Even in France in the first
War I never saw such filth. In front of everyone, too.

Filth.   Though she looked as
though she enjoyed it.
                Not me, no feels.
            Listen to her!
                        No, doesn't matter

age	79
marital status	widow
sight	65%
hearing	55%
touch	65%
taste	80%
smell	70%
movement	75%
CQ count	10
pathology	contractures; asthma; osteoporosis, mainly of limbs; inguinal hernia; bronchitis; osteo-arthritis; among others.

. . . we had then, good friends, who used to come and see us,
just drop in there and then, never mind what was happening,
once they nearly caught me and Ted on the job, oh, that was
comical!   We had to shout to them Hang on! while
he got his trousers up, but I went out and talked to them
without my drawers on, I just didn't put them on, and all
the while we were talking there was Ted sitting across from
me, knowing I had no drawers on, on tenterhooks as to whether
I should uncross my legs too boldly, but Len and Enid knew
what we'd been doing, I'm sure, though not that I'd left my
drawers off, and we all laughed and had a good time, oh, we
enjoyed ourselves in those days!   The
cocktails we used to get through!   Every week there'd
be a new recipe for a cocktail in my women's book and we'd
try it, invite the friends round to try the new one, oh those
were good times, the friends made up for not being able to

have children, and soon I began to prefer them, all the
trouble that children can be, I saw, and at least the
friends didn't have dirty nappies, though they were sick
in the bathroom sometimes, the friends, that was a mess to
clear up, wonder I'm not sick like that after food like
this, then she'd have another sort of mess to clear up
after me, then she'd have something to complain about, the
old bitch!

                               I've a good
mind to make complaints about her and this food she gives
us, to my friend on the Council, I still have friends –
all the treats of our Social Evening, indeed, just like
any night is what it'll be, as usual, give me a good book
any time, I just want to read.

                              There she is
again! Hurrying us up, I'd leave some of this if I wasn't
so hungry.   Never mind, Ivy, Doctor's coming
tomorrow, how I love him touching me!   Let
me try to work out a way so he has to touch me a lot when
he comes.

                        Difficult.

I'll think of something, come the morning.

    Last scrapings, horrible plates, not like the good
china I used to keep for best, not even like the everyday
stuff, either.

                  There, finished.

I'm finished, clear up, must help Sarah to clear away and
then I – oooh, my arm, the creaking, it gets set one way
and is so painful to move any distance at all after that,
aaaah picking up these plates

She's left more than usual.
All right, Sarah, don't wet your
knickers!
As soon as I've cleared up I'll get my book out and have
a good read, I do enjoy a good read, we are allowed books
here. If that Sarah will let me read, that is, chatter,
she does chatter, all emptiness, on and on. Not like my
old friends, all of them, dead now, as soon as we've cleared
I can get down to a – Now she's dropped it! Now she'll
be in trouble, I'm glad. That's it, give it to
her, silly old thing thinks she can move, ha ha ha ha ha!
the idea!

That dog. She's dotty over that dog.

Right, last things, clear
up, let's get started on the washing up, three volunteers
are better than an army of pressed tongue, as they used to
say, off we go, how's your father.

                    spoon,   spoon,
fork fork   spoon,
         knife,   fork,
   knife   here's a sticky one, who's been
doing what with this one?   The joys of
life, music while you work, used to listen regularly,
funny how radio's just died out, really, no one listens
like they used to, so quick, too.   Used to sing,
too, when we had friends round, to the piano, Ted could
vamp a little, we used to enjoy *strong*

> *Throughout old age, however long:*
> *If only we can cheerful stay*
> *And di-dum welcome every day.*
> *Not what we've been, not what we've done,*
> *What matters most is that we're* errrr
> *The joys of life continue strong*
> *Throughout old age, however long.*

> *The most important thing to do*
> *Is stay alive and see it through*
> *No matter if the future's dim*
> *For dum di dum, di dum di dim*
> *Oh, di di di, di di di deer*
> *OH, lucky us, that we are near!*
> *The most important thing to do*
> *Is stay di dum and see it through!*

She didn't notice, did she?   No sign!

Ah, a good sing-song does you no harm, no harm at all.

Yes, yes. Ivy this, Ivy that, why do I do her running around for her? Get the fancy goods boxes. Over in the cupboard. Right.

This glue is nasty. Paste rather than glue. Attracts the mice, I shouldn't wonder. And the rats!

Easy for her. Not so easy for some of us. Though I can do it all right. I can do more cracker cases in ten minutes than some of these can do in a whole evening. Not that I'm proud of it. Won't be able to read now until after we've finished work. What a pity. I do enjoy a good book.

Yes. I'll give out the work, carry round the boxes. *What were you doing yesterday, Mrs Ridge? Yes, this must be yours then. What about you, Ron?*

Here you are.   I can't help it
if you don't want to work, Mrs Ridge! Tell her,
not me. She's the one who makes you, not me.
                    And you! The cheek of it!
I don't have to do this, you know!

            Here.

                    Wake up, dear.
Yes, I knew it, there are mice dirts in the bottom
of the box, rolling around, sound as though they're
hard so they must have been rolling around here for
some time.   Filthy mice! Ugh! Mustn't tip
them out in front of this dotty old bugger George.
He'd only go out and eat them.
Though why not?   *Here you are,*
dear, stick this paper like she says, you know,
and here are some little sweeties for you, ho ho.

Yes, they've all got them now, madam.

Kept back the best brush and glue for myself, well,
I'm better at it than them. I can do more.

Now let's get two of them organised as I did

yesterday. A team or syndicate. That's the best
way, then we all get the most out of it. *Ron,
shall we do it the way we did it yesterday?*

*I know all about your arse, Ron, I know, I weep
for your poor old arse, but what can I do? If
you do the gluing at least you don't have to
go reaching all over the table for the roll
of paper, do you?   Come on now, Ron darling,
you know you'll only dwell on it otherwise, what
have you got to lose?*

*That's it, Ron, that's the ticket. Look, you have
this brush and glue, it's the best one, my one.
           Yes, the best. You'll be all right
with that, you'll do a good job, Ron.*

*Now what about you, Mrs Bowen, are you going
to join us as you did yesterday?*   Hope so, as
I'm not speaking to that bitch Ridge again, and
the other two are dummies.
*Certainly you can do the rolling again, dear,
Ron will do the gluing and I'll do the cutting.
So we've got three rollers between us and they
can keep going round, or rather back and forth
between you and Ron.
I'm sorry to seem to be ordering you around, but
someone has to do the organising, don't they?
Off we go, then.*
Hope Ron is going to be able to do the gluing

properly, it was his fault last time, he's the one
who should take the blame for what she was saying.
Keep my arms working and moving, so that they don't
get still and stiff and set, ah.
My book will have to wait until after this work has
finished, have to wait.

My eyes are not what they were, still, I collected
over seven hundred pound for the Blind Club, they'll
see to my eyes, for that, not seven hundred all at
once, of course, over the years, over the years,
silver paper from chocolate and milk bottle tops
and   other things.
That was when we were living near Southend. I could
have collected for the Lifeboat, but I preferred
to collect for the Blind. Ted did, too, he didn't
want me getting mixed up with that lot who collected
for the Lifeboat, there were some
unpleasant women amongst that lot, and men, too, and
Ted said he couldn't afford to get in with the wrong
lot, what with this new job that we'd gone down there
for in the first place, it was such a good job, a
chance in a million, and I thought he might be right,
and it turned out he was, after not so very long.
And he did so well as a rep for Stevensons, Ted, you
have to cultivate just the right sort of people in
that sort of job, and he was so successful at it that
within five years we moved out of Southend and had our
own little bungalow out at Thundersley, a new one, up

on the top of Bread and Cheese Hill, funny name,
all our friends used to remark on it, and laugh,
we had lots of friends then, they'd call round
just when they felt like it to see us, life
seemed so busy then, I joined the Women's Institute,
and did the flowers for the Church on the
rota, time seemed to fly by   doesn't
now

                        I'm getting so annoying
fat, through not working, not getting enough exercise
in this place. Still, all my life my weight
was slowly going up, all the time, all the more to
love, Ted used to say, bless him, oh!
Only time I came down a bit in weight was when they
cut my womb away, God knows what they didn't cut
away as well, saved my life, they said, but I've
never felt the same again, I've heard others say
that it made a new woman of them, but not me, I've
never been the same, I can truthfully say I miss
what they cut away, I'm not the same woman without
it. Oh, I'm alive, that was successful, yes, they
would call it a success.

*You're doing famously, Mrs Bowen. What a rate
we're going!   Oooh, I've made a rhyme!*

Ron, dear, could you please be a little more
sparing with the glue? You heard what House
Mother said about being careful, you know!
                                        His hands now,
I thought it was his arse, arthritis sounds like
it ought to be a disease of the arse really.
That's a comical idea, my Ted would have laughed
at that one!
Well, just try, Ron, you know what she's like
if she's crossed. For your own sake, not mine.

                    Good for you, Ron.

It was still like country out there then, that
was why we chose the bungalow there. One Sunday
afternoon while it was still being built we went
to a fair, it was a real country fair with local
people, not one of these shady travelling affairs,
here today and gone tomorrow, it was real old-
fashioned, it reminded me of when I was a little
girl. They even had that competition for children,
bobbing they called it, where they had to find a
sixpence with their mouths in an earthenware dish
filled with flour. Their faces, how everyone
laughed at their faces! I remember going in for
that myself when I was about six, and crying at not

winning, tears running through the flour on my
cheeks, until the man who was judging it sorted
out the sixpence with his fingers and gave it
to me to make up for not winning the prize,
which was half-a-crown, I think. A lot of money.
They also had a grinning match through horse-
collars, very old-fashioned that was, you don't
see that nowadays. It was so good to be back in
the country again, I was so glad that Ted had got
himself that job. I tried to be a good wife to
him, did special things for him to show that I
loved him, special things.

Then there were more bungalows
built, the country was creeping farther and farther
away, soon it meant getting in the car if
we really wanted to see the real countryside, we
were luckier than most in having a car at all, a
little Ford. We'd go out of a summer evening to
a country pub and have a drink, be quiet for a
change. You had to go quite a way, anyway, for
a drink, in Thundersley, as when they were build-
ing all those bungalows they forgot to build any
pubs, or shops too for that matter, I did hear the
land had belonged to some religious people or other
in the first place, who wouldn't allow the thought
of drink on their property, but that doesn't
explain why there were no shops. Soon people
began converting their front rooms into shops, and
Ted and I toyed with the idea at one time, to give

me something to do, as I was free of children, but
in the end we decided against it, no need, we were
comfortably off.
Clear up? That means Ivy clear up . . . I thought
so. *Yes, I will.* Here we go again. Don't finish
the one I'm doing, just bung it all in the box,
glue and all.   *Can I have yours, Ron, please?*
                    And Mrs Bowen?
                                    Ta muchly.
Let's put the finished ones in this empty box,
shall we?
                    Good. We've done a good
day's work, our lot. What about that old cow
Ridge's stuff?   Not much here. In fact
nothing at all.   Say nothing. Just collect the
glue and the paper and the scissors.
                        Oh! I wouldn't touch
you with someone else's bargepole, you dirty fat git!
                        You say that louder
so's she can hear, and you'll get the twitcher
again! Move away, quickly.

What about the dummies, what have they done?
Next to nothing. As usual   *What a mess,*
Mr Hedbury! As usual for him, too.
Yes, that's it, give her the twitcher, the slobbery
cow, the twitcher!
What a mess, Mrs Stanton!   Nothing. Ah well,
Ivy to clear up, as usual, as usual.
            Pile them away in the cupboard, anyhow.

Ah – that's
where the mice get in, through the wainscot there.
They must like this glue. Shall I tell her about
it? Not now. What's she on about? Pass the what?
I just want to sit down and get on with my book and
have a nice feel.
No chance of that now.
Oh, a relief to sit down again, a relief.
Scratch it, scratch my fan, relief too.
Now then, we're ready to
go. Sarah, then Charlie, then me.
I never win these things,
never have. *Here.* Don't even talk
to that cow Ridge. The lucky cow! The
music's stopped and she's got first go at opening
it! Music again. Snatch it and give it to Ron. *And
you! One of these days.* . . .

Sarah's got it. *Go on, Sarah, undo it!*
Not quite there.

Here it comes. Quickly to Ridge, quicker it goes the
sooner it'll come back to me – not while she's keeping
it though! *Pass the parcel!* That
shithouse again – wonder she's allowed in a good clean
House like this. Oh – Ron's got it undone. *What's
in it, Ron?*
Ha ha ha – shouldn't laugh, really. But
can't help it, ha ha. *She said you'd get a lovely
surprise, Ron! Ha ha ha ha ha! And you have, too!*

Ho ho ho!
Didn't we used to go at it!   What jousts we
had! Jousts, Ted used to call them, his prick a
great lance he'd charge me with, more like a pink
rubber truncheon it looked with its mackintosh on.
                         Takes a long while these days.
                                    Longer and
longer.   But we get there in the end.
                                       Always!

On the Readicut rug in front of the gasfire, that
was a good one, a particularly memorable one.
Long, that took long, but it was extra special
good when I did come. Chintz we had on the chairs
then, chintz was all the go in Southend at that time.
And making rugs at home. I'd made that rug from a
kit, they sent you all – Exercise?
Like a prison, this is. Exercise time. I like a
good walk, a tramp over the moors. Oh well, I can
finish later, I wasn't nearly there, anyway. Mrs
Stanton would like a push round, I'll do her,
sacrifice myself and feel good, because she
smells the worst.
Off we go!   Yes, she
does stink! *How are you, Mrs S?*
No answer. I've never heard her speak since I
came here. *CAN'T HEAR A THING, CAN YOU,
MRS STANTON?*   Poor old
girl. Wonder what she was when she was young?
Didn't prepare herself for this, obviously. I did.

When my Ted went I knew what was coming, so I
prepared myself for it. They say women live
longer than men because they never retire. Men
don't prepare themselves for retirement, as a
rule. It's their own funeral. Women are better,
anyway.
Push, how she's a weight. *DON'T GET ANY
LIGHTER, DO YOU, MRS STANTON?*
                                Puffs you out.
Ivy won't end up in a place like this, I said, Ivy
won't.
There we were, stuck on this little railway station,
in the middle of nowhere. Oh, you could read the
name of the place well enough, there were lights
on, I'll say that for them, but it didn't tell
you anything that mattered. And Ted blamed me
for not looking out for the place, and I blamed
him for wanting his little bit and tiring me
out so that I fell asleep. It was a carriage
with no corridors and we had a compartment to
ourselves, it was tempting at the time, we thought
why not, we were young then. And the only train
stopping at that time of night was going in the
opposite direction, so we had the choice of
nothing, since he had to be at work at nine sharp
the next day, but sleeping on the wooden benches,
and damn me if he doesn't want another bit there
and then, because he couldn't sleep, he said, and
it was so funny we both burst out laughing and it
was all right again.   Now she's dropped off.

The things I remember!   Push
her over there.   *All right, Mrs Stanton?*
Yes, she's all right.

Sport! More effort! No, I'm going to sit this
one out, she can't make me take part if I don't want
to, I'm going to read my book, here it – Ivy again,
fetch and carry, get the mops. All right, I'll get
the mops but then I'm going to sit down and get on
with my book.   One, two, wet. There.
                    And at least she thanks me.
Now where's my book?

                              Here.
              My marker, torn newspaper.   Ah,
"A bus is not caught by either my father or myself,
a number eleven, that is, the one we came by, on
our return. We walk down the whole length of North
End Road. We always do this. We enjoy the street
market. Occasionally my father buys something.
Usually it is vegetables. Today he buys some Felixmeat for the dog. The dog is a perverse dog.
Felixmeat is his delight, nothing can make earth
seem more like heaven than Felixmeat, in his view.
I feel it is fortunate that not more of us have
views like this.   I catch with my father a
number twenty-seven bus several minutes after arriving
at the bus-stop in Hammersmith Road at the end
of North End Road. The northern end of North End
Road, that is. We could have caught a number nine
or a number seventy-three, to place them in numerical

order, had either of these splendid numbers been
opportune. But we catch. . . ." What a load of old
rubbish! No story about it. Boring.

Where's my other book?

Ah.   "There was no doubt that Polly
Mallinson was dead. Indeed, there was no doubt that
Polly Mallinson had been murdered. But the mystery
was why anyone should have gone to such enormous
pains to murder her in such a complicated way and
to have her found in such a crowded place.

Ascot racecourse lies about twenty miles
to the south-west of London in pleasant wooded
country that is, alas, fast being eaten into by the
commuter octopus that is the metropolis. Each year
in the month of June the Ascot Gold Cup meeting is
held there, a race which attracts horses of the very
best bloodstock in the world to compete against each
other. It equally attracts the best human bloodstock to be found in London during that sunny month,
the cream of which clusters into that holy of holies
called the Royal Enclosure.   On this particular Gold Cup day the race was won by Garlic
Clove by a head from Hiatus with Noseylad three
lengths behind, and as Sir William Scadleigh, K C V O,
P C, D S O and Bar, relaxed from the tension of watching
the finish at the crowded rail he became fully aware
of a pressure on him from behind which was natural
during the race but hardly necessary now it was over.
Reacting firmly but in a manner befitting an officer
and a gentleman, he gently eased back. The pressure

ceased, and as Sir William turned he was astounded
to see what had caused it. It was a young girl,
scarcely out of her teens, and she was falling. As
he automatically reached out to grasp her arm and
save her he became aware of several things simul-
taneously: that she was wearing very nearly nothing,
that *rigor mortis* had set in anything up to forty-
eight hours previously, and that before she died
someone had been treating her very inconsiderately
indeed." This is better, know where you are when
it's telling you a story.   "It was not
possible to tell what colour Polly's eyes might
have been, for they were now only enlarged, bloodied
sockets. Sufficient remained of her hair, however,
to establish that it was almost cert – " Laugh! Now
what's she on about? Stupid. *Ha ha.*
"Sufficient remained of her hair, however, to establish
that it was almost certainly red-gold. It was also
fairly certain that whoever Polly had annoyed enough
to cause to treat her in this way was a smoker, for
he or she had stubbed out innumerable cigarettes all
over her.   Not normally a man who could be
easily shocked – he had seen too much of war and its
horrors for that – Sir William gasped as much as any
other member of the crowd which quickly gathered
round what was left of poor Polly Mallinson. Their
idle curiosity was quickly ended by the arrival of two
St John's Ambulancemen who covered the body with a
blanket and summoned the racecourse police.
              There was another reason why Sir William

was more shocked than perhaps he might
otherwise have been: for Polly was his –'' *Oh!*
         oh!   oh!   House Mother's angry!

Sorry, I'm sorry, I'll pay attention! Have to
be careful now, or I'll be out. Don't want to
cause trouble. That's why I'm here, they trans-
ferred me from Ravensholm because they said I was
a troublemaker. That wasn't all.   Can't
look after myself, can I? Nearly froze to death
last time I was on my own. Would have done if that
young fellow from down below hadn't come about the
wet coming through the ceiling.   Fair pair of
knockers on her.   *Hooray!* That'll show her
I'm still paying attention.   Could have
had one together if I'd started again sooner.

        In London one summer, it was one of the times
he was on leave, very hot day, he took me to a
night club, forget where it was. Didn't see much
in it, myself, nor did he. Did a strip for him
myself that night in the boarding house, much more
for him to enjoy. Oh, I was keen on it then! What
would Ted say if he saw me today? He's well out
of it, that's certain, well out of it. And he
didn't have to bear much pain, either, except
right at the very end.

                        Doggie, doggie,
doggie. Must cost a lot to feed a great brute
like that.   How much? Pounds and pounds a
week.   This must be it now.   Yes.

I could do it like that, once. Used to, often.
Don't really miss it now, any more. What is it?
What is it to miss?
        Listen to her!
                No, doesn't matter

age	81
marital status	widower
sight	30%
hearing	45%
touch	55%
taste	40%
smell	40%
movement	45%
CQ count	8
pathology	contractures; dehydration; incipient hypochromic anaemia; incontinent; inguinal hernia; inoperable rectal carcinoma; among others.

. . . again. The same again.   It's
not as though they tempted me
to eat and risk the agony down
below.

                         Cutting down
has helped, I was right. The
only way not to inflame the piles
is not to eat. Found that out
first time I had them. Don't
feel any weaker, I was weak to
start with.   Must eat something, though, to show
them, told them I was not a big eater, don't want to be thrown
out, not on the streets again, couldn't take it, the ramp, those
dirty   Soup is what I should have, a man in my –
She's taking my dinner!   She can have it. . . .
                    No, the House Mother shouldn't hit

her like that, that twitcher is a wicked

    t w i t c h e r
Say nothing, hurts to m o v e, p e c k a t t h i s
                I d o n't w a n t it,
w e a k e n s y o u, AH! m y r i v e t e d a r s e,
aaaa!   f e e l s l i k e n o t h i n g,
             I c a n t h i n k
of n o t h i n g b u t t h e p a i n a t t h e
v e r y c e n t r e o f m y a r s e.

S a y   n o t h i n g

      K e e p q u i e t

   B e a r t h e p a i n w i t h o u t

s a y i n g

Soon   have   to   move
again

                                        aaaa!

                                   Dropped it, she
has.   Mess, mess, it's all a mess. I'd let
the dog eat it, easiest way to clear up that sort of mess.
                                        Tad would
have cleared it up in no time, Taddie would.
                          He was a fine dog, Tad, broke my
heart when he had to be put to sleep, there was more of
me in that dog than there was in myself at that time.
                          They could never understand
it, the way   I   loved   that

Oh, the song, must make
some   effort
        she   must
    see me singing
            of life continue strong
        Throughout   old age, however long
        If only we can   cheerful
stay, And   every day.
                not what we'll
    What matters most   that we're free
        joys of life continue strong
    Throughout old age, however long.

        Important   to do
        stay alive
    No matter if   future's

        knows best, and brings good cheer AAA!
the pain shoots again
                        again!

                                          Work, no, that
will mean moving. No matter how still I try to
keep my arse, if my hands are moving then it
gives me gyp, *aaaa*, there.

                                          Careful?
How can you be careful with her scrappy bits
of paper when your arse is giving you gyp all
the time?   You can't keep your mind
on anything, can you?

                              Just a smear
along one edge, sounds
easy, but she doesn't take
into account my fingers
aren't what they used to
be, with this arthritis
liable to finish them off
altogether if – *Yes, I don't care.*

That woman's
language! They are the gentle sex, they say.
Some of them.

Oh. I'll
try to work, then, it may take my mind off of
it, my arse, though I doubt it, I doubt it very
much.
The red paper, this isn't the
roller I had yesterday, mine was newer than this,
this is grubby.   That slimy old
woman must have been using it, getting her
filthy spittle all over it!   Ugh!
But don't complain, never
complain about such a
small thing. Never com-
plain about the small
things. Get on with it.

aaaaaaaaaah, the pain shoots, shoots!

I can't Ivy, it's my arse, I'm in constant pain from it. There's no words to describe it.

Whether I work or not I still get it, nothing I
can do makes it any the easier.
                              Nothing to lose.
You're right, Ivy, I've nothing to lose, nothing.

The best one? Can't think what state the others
must be in, then. Have a look.
Yes, the others look pretty lousy, all glued up
and bristles coming out and dirty. For small
mercies.

I'll just finish this one on my own.

There's   no   satisfaction
in   it,   in   any   of   it,   now.

                Off we go.

Sloppity glue.
                    In the mind, mind the
pain shooting up my! Went to the doctor. Piles,
he said at once. No, I've had them, not the same
this time. No, he said, doctors know best. Must
ask her if I can see the doctor sooner than Thurs-
day. Can't wait till then. She'll not like it,
she hates anyone making a fuss. I can't do it!

       I can't wait, either, till Thursday.

K e e p   q u i e t   a b o u t   i t ,   t h e n .

    Ivy understands about my problem, would make
someone a good wife, still, Ivy. Nothing to look
at, of course, she doesn't even seem to have that
look of peace that some of the other women have.
Did she have a hard time of it?
                    There's no telling.

Still hurts to glue, I still have to move even
ever so slightly. How can I think about anything else, it's constant, the pain, what else
is there to think about, it goes round and round
in circles, my mind, off it, on it, not very
often off it.

Luxury bed, downy pillows, none of your plastic-
filled articles.   Out,
out, he said, and out he took it, left a gap
at the back of my mouth, felt like a bomb
crater, kept poking my tongue in it, all salty
blood, you can't help it, can you?
                                             S t r a y,
s t r a y,   s t r a y.
And then you don't know where you are. Still
don't understand how he swindled me on that deal,
just know he definitely did swindle me. I paid
him three hundred for the whole consignment, and
somehow when I got it it was only a consignment
for which I would have paid one-eighty, if that,
two hundred at the most.   His
name was Flannery or Chinnery or something like
that, a sharp one he was, he could swindle you
so's you had no way of getting back at him, offices

he called it – *Yes?*

More careful still?
*My hands, this arthritis, Ivy, I'm being as
careful as I can, really I am.* Not very
interested, anyway, balls to it, nothing makes
the pain any better, don't make one any better
concentrating on the other, aaaaaaaaah!

Yes, I know what she's like when she's crossed.
Yes, Ivy, I'll try. Don't want to cross House
Mother.

Then there was that
sneaky little sod who also had one of the railway
arches down there behind the Broadway, he could
drop you in the fertilizer too if you weren't very
careful, though with him you could see it coming
and you could watch out for it. And never deal
with him unless you had to. The best way was to

play safe and sell before you had bought. Make
sure you had a sale before you paid for whatever
it was. Even then you could get caught sometimes,
find yourself *aaaaaaaaah!*
Not again, I could do with a better cushion than
this, she ought to provide an air cushion for
people in my condition, I've even seen people take
them on buses, if they were in this painful condition, what can I do, only ask, and I'm afraid to
do that.

       M o r e   g l u e
              Mrs Bowen, can you pass me
your glue, please? This one's finished.

Thanks very much, Mrs Bowen.
         Yes, all right now.

       T h e r e   m a y   b e   o t h e r s
l i k e   m e .   I   h o p e   s o .   I   h o p e
n o t ,   o n   t h e   o t h e r   h a n d .   I
w o u l d   n o t   w i s h   i t   o n
         t h e m .

Finish,
finish now. Didn't do much to take my mind
off of it. A little. A very little.
Still, it's something. A little something.
She's all right,
that Ivy. A good sort.   Finish this last
one, nice and tidy.
Yes, here it is, Ivy. They're nice and tidy
today, aren't they, Ivy?

Try again. *They're better today, Ivy?*
No proper answer.
Well, I think they're better than yesterday's.
And considering all the circumstances, too. Let
them complain. That's it, until they complain
then I don't care.

Ivy and that Mrs Ridge are always having a go
at each other. Stupid bastards, the pair of them.

We're the best, we are.
That's all right, then, that's a relief. Forgot
my arse for just two minutes

aaaaaaaaah!

Pass the Parcel! What a
waste of time, more movement, but
Pass the parcel, up my arcel!
oooooooooooooh! My arse again, keep still,
keep still   A fart would be a
blessing   D a r e n' t.

Ooooooh, *no!* The pain, pain!

Pass the parcel.
Chuck the bleeding thing.

But what's in it? Sarah's getting it open. Now
it's off again.
Curiosity.

It's my turn, that old woman's cheating! *Pass it on!*
No need to chuck it at me!   It's stopped,
it's me, I can get it undone, I'll win, what is it?
SHIT!   It's a parcel of shit! Is that
what I've won? Is that all?   Stinking shit!
shit shit shit shit shit shit shit shit shit shit shit
shit shit shit shit shit shit shit shit shit shit shit

shit!

w h y?

                    Get up,
she wants us to take exercise. Take up thy
arse and walk?   I'll try,
the pain can't be worse
                aaaaaaachk! Yes it can!

            But try again.
T o   w a l k.   The pleasure of it. As
I stroll along the promenade. It must be a tidy
middling.   The trouble
with business is that you can think you're doing
so well and then you get caught for a tidy
packet. Right into the middling, right into the

fertilizer.   It may be something to do
with the way I walk, of course. That may have
something to do with it.
H a e m o r r h o i d s   o r   p i l e s :
j u s t   a s   t h o u g h   y o u   c o u l d
c h o o s e !   *aaaeh!*
I shall try again to remember my first fuck.
The first is the one you never forget, they say.
They are not right in my case, not for the first
time, either. Yet I remember it was when I was
seventeen, because that was what I said when
questioned about it some time later. But who it
was is difficult to remember.   Who did I
know at seventeen? It must have been someone from
the town, I would not have been stupid enough to
shit on my own village doorstep, as we say in the
trade. In that case, it might have – No, I can't
walk any more, I must sit and be damned to her
and her dog.

If that seed had borne fruit, I should have a child
of over sixty now. It might have been a son, a
competitor. Tom was never a competitor, none of
them. I was their father, and I saw I remained so,
oh yes!
Who could it have been? My memory's playing me up
again, so she was redhaired, ginger-eyed and had
a pair of tits on her like twin mountains and an
arse as broad as East Anglia. Her fanny was like

a red ravine, dry and dusty, not so dusty.
                          Her face?
I can't remember her face.

                               Ah, yes,
that was fun last time, the tourney. I enjoyed
it. Wonder if I can get a bet on this time? Mrs
Bowen won easily, I'll back her.   *Mrs Ridge,*
I'll bet you my breakfast milk that Mrs Bowen wins.

        But what will you give me if I win?

                      Right, you're on. Shake.
Now I've got a bet on.
                    They're at the tapes!
Come on Mrs Bowen! Lot depends on Charlie pushing,
too.   *They're*
off!

Hooray! One up to me!

                              They're off
again! *Come on Charlie!*

Rah! Two up!   I shall win!

              They're off! Last time, I must
win two-to-one at least!
                              Rah!
Cheers for Mrs Bowen and Charlie! You owe me a feel,
Mrs Ridge, a feel, tonight!

She gets it both ways, she does. If she'd've
won she'd've got my breakfast milk, as it is she
gets a feel she'll enjoy just as much as I will,
more, probably, with my arse in this state. That's
funny, forgot it during the tourney. Just goes
to show, just goes to show.
                    But it's getting worse now, it's
paying me back, aaaaoooh!
                    ooooooooooh!   *aaOOh!*
No, try to think of something to take my mind off
it, the feel, that's something to look forward to,
ooooooooh, b u t   i t' s   n o   h e l p   n o w,
w h a t   s h a l l   I   d o?

              S t a r t e d   w h e n   I
w a s   f i f t y - t w o,   i t' s   a
p u n i s h m e n t   f o r   t o s s i n g   o f f
t h a t   l i t t l e   b o y   w h e n   I   w a s
i n   t h e   N a v y,   i t' s   a
p u n i s h m e n t,   b e   s u r e   y o u r   s i n s
w i l l   f i n d   y o u   o u t.

He asked for it, he was a saucy little sod, and I
paid him a few piastres.

              aaaaooaoaoah!

aaaaaah!

                    oooooh!

oooaaaeh!

eaeaell!

*ooooo*ooh*, oooh, aaaah!*

eh!

oooooooooch!

ooooooooooooeoeosososoaoeo!

aaaaajjja!

    we never did think we'd live to see him grow
up! I'll force myself to think of something else.
      we never did   to see
think we never did
                 we'd live
     a few piastres seemed
so little at the time, for what
it   was
    years after, that smell

                    City of galloping
knobrot

                    oooooh!

ooooooooaoah!
                    this can't go on surely
something must bust it must give the pain over
it must make me bust   *ooooooooooh!*
          ooooooorh!

one two three four one two three four sheep over
the edge one three six ten fuck them all *oooooo*

                    n o t h i n g   c o m e s
o f   i t ,   n o t h i n g   s e e m s   t o
h e l p ,   y o u ' d   t h i n k   t h e y   w o u l d
b e   a b l e   t o   d o   s o m e t h i n g
f o r   y o u ,   p e o p l e   h a v e   b e e n
s u f f e r i n g   f r o m   s o r e   a r s e -
h o l e s   s i n c e   t i m e   b e g a n .

                    no, *oooooh!*

oooooooooooooh!
                    R e g u l a r ,   i t
c o m e s   i n   w a v e s .

ooooooooooooooooooooooh!

ooooooough!

                              oooodh!
                 OOOOOOOH!

      Listen to her!

            No, doesn't matter

age	85
marital status	not known
sight	45%
hearing	55%
touch	30%
taste	20%
smell	60%
movement	45%
CQ count	6
pathology	contractures; plantar fasciitis; mental confusion; progressive senile dementia; cholecystitis; osteoporosis; among others.

. . . me and then   get this down me and
then I'll   be all right
                         spuds and mashed and   with knees
try hard   peas, peas, peas
shovel peas in, more   then I'll be all right
            more?

                                              more
            general sold his   cockerel
                         the meat is good, more meat, that's
the thing, must eat to get right, get this down me and then
I'll be all right, that's it, ask for more meat. *More meat?*

He's not going to eat his, no, I'll have his, must eat, how he
can leave it I don't know, here Oh!   twitcher!
            no . . .   *eee!* my hands,

the backs of my hands!   Hurts   not for long, I've
got over worse, I'm the toughest.
                        They said it was just a craze,
wanting to eat, it would never   catch on, la la la!
Catchy.
                                I always did believe
in ruining your own work, it was one of my fondest beliefs,
if you do that then you don't have to beholden to somebody,
do you?

    Scrape the plate, the mash off, mash off corners

                                Swinging on
ropes, nothing much on, just something round his
                        unmentionables, as we
used to call them, into all that mucky water and crawlies,
out in the bare colds or   rocks was it,
only a picture after all.
                Another one I saw had Charlie Chimpanzee
in it, when I was that high.   Then we had Gilbert
Harding being rude, we enjoyed it! Diving into the
crawlies and the water all covered by scrum, those jungle
creepers!   How we used to laugh!
                She ought to show us films here,
though some would abuse the privilege, they never do.
                It would never do.

                            da-da, ma-ma

                    Brisket and taters, brisket, brisket

atrisket, my love bisquit, brown bread and waistcoat,
crumbs to his watch-piece.

My name's Gloria, Glory
for short. It's too far this time.   May I never?
My true love went once round fingering, blue hair he
had with his long black eyes, four foot   three
in his bloomers, I remember him so clearly, it was in
a pub we first met, I was with my mates at the time, he
was with his.   Yellow jumper and pale skirt
This for two or more I was with him,
standing in the dark. Milk stout was all our tipple, then.
He was my first, it was raining at the time.

She's in trouble this time, not me, House Mother'll hit
her, not me, this time

No, she's
not, that's not fair, she's only getting a tonguelashing,
not the twitcher, it's not fair   not fair!

me
me me meeee memememememememememe! say it aloud
ME!   The twitcher, lucky
she didn't hear, lucky me!

            A gallon of gin I must have
drunk last night, this won't do, where's the money
coming from?   It doesn't get him anywhere.
I must cut down on the food, supporters and sus-
penders, it won't do, I won't have his drinking though
I'll have his drink *been, no twat you'll be,*
    What matters most is what we'll be
    The joys of life continue strong
    Throughout old age, however long.

. . . MOST IMPORTANT THING TO DO
IS STAY ALIVE AND SEE IT THROUGH
NO MATTER IF THE FUTURE'S DIM
JUST KEEP STRAIGHT ON AND TRUST IN HIM
FOR HE KNOWS BEST AND BRINGS GOOD BEER
OH LUCKY US THAT WE ARE HERE!
THE MOST IMPORTANT THING TO DO
IS STAY ALIVE AND SEE IT THROUGH!
                        Now she ought to be
pleased with me, no twitcher, no one can sing louder
than I can, not even that fat slob Ivy, cow.

Work! The people must
work if they are to earn their daily bread!   Life
is not all butter, someone has to earn the guns as
well, ha ha!

What's she
giving them two to do? I could do it, whatever it
is. *Here!*   Twitcher! The twitcher!

It's not only that, there are tripes and lazy
breeders for supper, summer in a sauce made of milk
and parsley.

I think, I think!

Careful,
I'm always careful, never let them stick it up me
without a rubber on, very careful all my life,
never had no kids, never!   Very careful,
very clever, that's me.
I can do that easy,
that crinkly paper's not very good for it though,
not very good at it.   Nasty work,
only fit for the Ivys.   *Nothing, nothing, nothing.*
Nothing!   Not my box, hate this
work, nothing here, who makes me?

Don't want this work. *Don't want this work!* Or
this Ivy, cow she is, slummocky old cow.

Slummocky old shit cow!   That annoyed
her, that'll teach her to order me about, I'm
not here to be ordered about!   Except
by the twitcher, that's all that keeps me quiet,
the only thing.

I'll just sit here, that's what I'll do, just sit
here, and only work if I feel like it. Start one,
roll the paper round the roller, here, this isn't
as easy, roller roller penny a paint, painy a
pent, old cow, I'll roller, red paper, red paint,
red roller roller roller.
And just leave it like that. Then anyone who
sees me will think I've just broken off for a
moment.   Oh, I'm clever, you know, I
know all the dodges, I learned them, all the
dodgers, when I was working, you learn all the
dodgers to work as little as
                    This way I won't have to touch
the horrible glue, no, not even to touch it.

                    The twitcher's
gone up the stage with her, the twitcher has, bye

bye the twitcher, good riddance twitcher! If
I just sit here and keep quiet and do nothing
then she won't come down here again with the
twitcher for me, the twitcher for me, If
ye're no a garlic, the twitcher's for me.

If possible keep on going where   they
are all like   Mind you, if I was her I
would not put up with any of it, any of it, myself

It pays to keep up with your payments. Sometimes
we wouldn't. They were all away. The girls had
it away. No one played at home, then.

She's going to team up with those two! Now they
won't talk to me. It's not fair. Yesterday she
did it, too. She deliberately doesn't ask me. I'm
sure of that. I can do this as well as anyone,
round the roller, the glue. I could be part of the
team.   It hurts.

Where are they all gone? I had them here, all of
them.   And now they're not here. It may

be my true love, my one true love. His hair was
golden, his eyes were blue, he stood six feet two
in his bare socks, the first one. My one true.
One two, dozens since then. He bumped into me
coming out of the four ale bar into the corridor,
there I was scrubbing near the milk stout. I was
a young girl then. He was my first. Swept me
off my feet. Swept my chimney, he called it, my
black chimney. What could I say? It was a
frosty morning. Frost clears away the flu and does
good for England. Everything's in a mess

That time they let me play. Let the piccaninny join
in! that Bobbie yelled. I enjoyed it more than my
tapioca.
                    What would you say if I
took off my arm and gave it to you in a stew?
              Got you there, got you there!
                    Why not?

It was the milkman and his wife who ruined it.
What made him marry a mad woman?   The cream
curdled all, she would and all.

So instead of
doing nothing, you would rather do nothing! I
spit at you. That Ivy is a slummocky swine.
Her tits hang down. In really, you can't see
her tits, she just has a bulge. She's got no
tits, a long streak of gravy. What that Ivy
has done to me! How many times have I had
hot dinners than hot times? Where do they all
come from? She pinched my last piece of meat,
the piece I had been saving, she did, that Ivy.
But jesus will come for my end. He will lift
Me up into his heavenly boudoir and I will sing
with the angels all the night long. The stars
will shine down on Me when he comes, his Milky
Stout, and the sun will come out and beam upon
the starry firmament. And we shall all live
happily ever after ever until the end amen.
Aah, isn't that nice.   Except for Ivy,
she'll not have an end, she'll go on with her
gravy tits and sticky fingers all her life
until she dies and

Well well well! They can talk!

And what about the price of candles! A girl can't
go on and on burning her wick at both ends, can
she?   When
will we be allowed to see what really goes on?
Yesterday they won the war, all the Tommies came
home raving for it. Their only pride was between
their legs, like a dog's tail. We worked over-
time. No fear of that, I said, when he came, I've
been a good girl, after my way, always fashionable,
I was, wore a hooped crinoline sort of dress,
starched sleeves, bare arse. Oh, we were proudish
then!

Now when I try to brush up my brushing, it hurts
under my armpit, hurts. I should go to the doctor.
He'll help me, the doctor in Margery Street. Walk
up through Exmouth Market, buy some priest shoulder
at a stall, then up past that place in Amwell
Street that always smells of flux, opposite the
other church, and down into Margery Street, rest
my feet. Good doctor, he is, he'll heal my armpit,
nasty nagging pain and then it comes sharply, ouch!
Or some smoked salmon scraps, not shoulder, only

a tanner a quarter, bits off the edges,
bones, scraps, one of my fondest favourites,
smoked salmon scraps from Exmouth Market, chew
them, get the bits out, just as good as they
pay earth for, lots more.
                                   Hungry again, nothing
more till breakfast, there's worst to come.

My one true, love. His hair was ravenblack, his
eyes were green, he stood four foot three in
his bare, the first one. My one two. One true,
several since then. He jostled me in the public
bar when I was a scrubber. I must have been
forty by then, a mere. The milk stout I remember
coming out of quart bottles. No one must know.
How many beans since then? There must have been,
one after one after one after one after one after
one, no   *No!*

These things make us all. Try for the sky. Jesus
will. Not in here you won't. Was jesus a shep-
herd? Did they have sheep in the desert? He could
make food for them, fish and bread, wish he could

make me some now, I'm hungry. They don't feed
us here. In my day I'd pop down the shop on the
corner for a quarter of Wall's luncheon meat and
a tin of peas. That's a good feed.
What's she at now? Is she coming down here again,
yes.   But not the twitcher, ha, she's left
the twitcher up on the stage.   Good.

Here comes horrible Ivy creeping down the table!
Ivy the creeper, after the work. They must be
finished. Haven't done any. Who cares, who cares?
Can't make me work. Just try it!
                     Ivy the creeper-
crawlie, can't touch me!

You are a stinky woman!

         Twitcher's up on the stage, meeeeahr!
Now she'll come to me next, without her twitcher.
              Now.
              Why should I work?

                         Leave
me, leave me!   While there is no pie
we make hay, six times seven sends you to heaven,
whompot, whompit, whampit!   It was a lively
leading lido when we first could greet groaning the

great dawn green with grassy longings, if only I
could now, how now how how?
　　　　　This must be enough to be going on with,
there's always tomorrow, after all, always – Pass
the Parcel, what's this, I love games. Pass the
Parcel and I'm the winner, the postman brings me
a parcel, brown paper, must be mine, I'm a winner,
post today, late for Christmas, make sure I'm the
one who gets the lovely surprise at the end. Something to look forward to!
Off we go!

　　　　Next to me, me!　　　Parcel for me!
　　　　　　　Open it, the music's stopped. Feels
soft, strip off the paper. What can it be?
Music.　　Oh.　　*You bastard sod!*
Cow woman Ivy, answering back, she always on my
back! Get off my back, you cow Ivy!

　　　　　　　　　　　Next to me!
Here again. Stink. What is it?
Hold on to it. Unwrap some more. Yes, stink.
Rules?　　　　　　　　　*All right, have it!*
I won't be interested in your game any more, won't
play any more.　　　Stinking rotten game. Whose
game do you particularly, the long ones, I could
always give rise to a long long one, it was my
speciality in those days.　　　Madam had four in
her room, she would give one to us girls as a

favour, she would, and I was always the most
special favourite, I was, I was, I was, I was,
I was, I was, I was, I was, I was, I was, I was,
I was, I was, I was, was, was,

was!

All the bees, bottom, bum, behind, buttocks,
ARSE!
I know what killed him, I know what killed him
that night, too much of a good thing, that's
what killed him, heart attack during the night
the doctor called it, but I know it was too
much of a good thing that killed him.
                        He was a good husband to me,
I had eighty children by him, too much of a good
thing done for him in the – Now what?

Travel!

          I hate exercise.   But
the twitcher!

Ooooh, so fat I can hardly move. Waddle,
waddle, what's it matter now, don't have to
attract the fellers any longer, so what's it
matter? More a job to keep them away, ha ha!
Ha ha, that Ron, ha!

Round.   Round. Keep away from that
stinking Ivy. One of these days she'll bring
me to such a point that I'll forget myself and

dot her one where she won't like it at all, no.
           Where no one likes it.

My true love's hair was red, red as the dawn,
my one true love. His eyes were brown, he stood
four foot umpteen in his boots. My one two,
three four, who's counting? Ha ha! I bumped
into him as I was sloshing the floor in the
Gents. He stumbled over my bucket and there we
were on the floor, at it among the Jeyes and
Lysol. He swept me off his feet. I was quite a
young thing then, stout with it, I enjoyed it,
who'd have thought it, in those days?

          That Ron has sat down, so
shall I, twitcher or no twitcher, she must give
it him first, if she's fair, the twitcher, he
sat down first, Ron.

We waved and waved as he went by, King George the
Sixth, they let us off dirty to wave from the
upper windows, it was so exciting, us girls, it
turned me over, truly it did, waiting for hours

we were in the hot sun, it was late December.
And the banners were out, we waved our union
jacks, and cheered and cheered. It was quite
good. That was at the time when I was afraid I
might become Queen myself one day – no
twitcher if she's going to run a tourney, good.

What's that? *Your breakfast milk? Yes, I'll bet
you, Ron.*   *All I've
got that you'd want, Ron, is a quiet feel in the
toilet before bed.*
Shake.
         Two lots of breakfast milk for me, yes,
always too many cornflakes and not enough milk,
that'll be nice, something real nice to look forward
to. There they go.

Silly old fool   got himself hit.

And again! Won't get me two lots. Never mind.
I'll get a feel.

Three times! Ron certainly backed the right one.
         You shall have it, Ron, never fear, you

shall have it. Wonder what he'll feel? My
twat is favourite, or at least it used to be.
Or perhaps he wants me to hold his horrible.
Or bag of creepy skin?   Anyway, it'll
be short, Ron, I'll promise you that.
       No, shan't listen! Bung
my ears up!

      This big meat pie, so big
you could hardly get yourself round it. So big.
Three of us made it together, for the Club. In
those days they let you, and my friend Edie got
me together with all this lard and flour. It
must come soon. Bought lots and lots of meat,
very expensive. For the upper crust we had sea-
gulls, and this tower like the Eiffel Tower it
was in the middle. It held up the crust very
nicely with just a little point sticking out.
Ooooh, it did taste nice! Wasn't there none left
over for the curates?
      We were good in those days, in spite
of that rationing. You had to be good to get
anything off of grocers and suchlike. They had
a marvellous time of it, having it off in the
back stores.
Where are they now, the martins and perhaps?

All dead. No Edie, Frank, Johnnie, Doug, Maeve,
Dil, no, none of them.

Where do they all go? Where are they now? Where
am I now?   How can all these things be here,
and not them?   That would be a
curious caper, as he used to say
              I asked for a job once, where are
your references, they said   You've
got to have the right pieces of paper, you see,
at the time you want the
I want a jobbies

It is very confusing, laughing

                          Laugh! Laugh,
laugh, I nearly   died
              We went round the halls
one night, lead in his pencil, more like a great
big   His blood pressure was high, laugh,
you never saw anything like it !   We
were in a box, boxes of chocolates, programmes,
as many cigarettes as you could eat. A very good
show but I know what he was after with his great
purple pen !
Like a lick of my seaside, he would say.

                      I would

        In the first place there were too many
there, in the third it was neither here nor

there but underneath, where we all liked it,
underneath, pass me the deeoyleys, she would say,
just like that, pass – Good! That Ivy's getting
it! It's a change, give her the *twitcher*, House
Mother!   Now she's in trouble, bitch Ivy,
fat slummy greasy Ivy! Fatty Ivy chop, buy them
at the family butcher's.

                       So what?
She's giving us the benefit, again.   Lovely,
have it off, let's all see

                              Oh, she
threw her clothes over the dog!
                       Now the other
       that's it
                 Oh, I always enjoy this
bit, it reminds me of the old days when I was out
working. . . .   How far now?

            Oops!
              They're all off, all,
Hoorah!
          Never with a dog, we went to the
Dogs' Home to choose one but came away without one,
I couldn't have kept it   anyway
          My new dress is stained with custard.
Who did that, now?   It must have been that
Ivy, I know it was that Ivy!   *Cow!*
Custard cow, taking no notice, getting her own back
because my tits are better than hers, custard cow,

cowardy custard cow.   True love, blue
eyes, green, six foot if an inch, he was tall as
well with it, scrubber I was, the first, first
        Listen to her!
               No, doesn't matter

age	89
marital status	widow
sight	50%
hearing	40%
touch	35%
taste	55%
smell	45%
movement	20%
CQ count	8
pathology	contractures; diabetes mellitus; colonic diverticulitis; benign renal carcinoma; lesion of alimentary tract; paraplegia; among others.

. . . tasty

                meat then

        that house, the kitchen itself could seat
twenty of us, did at Christmas before we served them, it
was warmer than the   servants' hall, that word worries
me still, always hated to think of myself as a servant, he
didn't, almost revelled in it, he did, knew his place and that
was a servant's place, indeed   this custard,
slop   and greens, how can she, in that   kitchen
there were great bowls we broke the eggs into for custard,
real custard, the arm you needed to beat that many would fell
an ox, two of us girls would take turn and turn about, sometimes my arm hurt so much that   that kitchen
was so big twenty of us could   the
mahogany cupboards, sets of drawers with brass handles, how
I hated brass, a waste to have brass to keep clean, but then

he would say it was good

                          my soul indeed,

what he was interested in was not my soul

                the old sod

with his great stomach, the stomach he had on him

                           Why not, he said,

        Because not, I told him

              The stomach on him, he'd be round the
kitchen spooning out the leavings in the big oven trays,
laughing if Cook or anyone tried to stop him, dodging round
and knocking things over with his great stomach and fat
                             arse.   I know.

There was too much room in that kitchen, Cook used to say,
even when she had to cook for sixty, there were that many
guests there on occasion, oh dear me   yes

           The mahogany cupboards, the whole range to
blacklead, eggs to beat, the meringues the sisters liked
too much, we used to put the yolks in scrambled eggs the
next morning, it was the best way to use them up.

               Years afterwards

went into Town one week and there he was, years after,
outside the Bear, his great stomach even bigger
              grinning
        I felt my insides twist, I couldn't help

myself, he had the effect on me.

                         In summer the sun used to beat down
on the range, it used to make it that hot
                         working there, double.

                                             My name is
Sioned, I work here, you're a pretty thing

                         How could I see it coming?

Clear up now, I'll help, I can still move, you know, push
at the wheels, I'll help, get the plates together, there,
lift – Oh no !   *I didn't mean*
to drop them, Miss!

                                   I wouldn't try to
feed the doggie, you've told us not to.

                         Yes, I deserve it.

cah, cah, cah   Goats
in the paddock, there. We had goats, then, never ate it
ourselves, but the sisters did. I never liked it, I wasn't
squeamish, no, but the sisters

                              No,
I won't sing her song. I think it's silly, so
she can do the other thing.

        As though it mattered, it wasn't my fault,
no, they can clear up on their own, a little mess
like that.

            What matters most

                    old age   *long* ha ah ah!
ha ha ha ha ha!

                    future's dim
                        hymn

            most important thing
                        through
ha ha! Nearly choked then.
                    I think it's so silly, they
can all go and do the other thing, I'm tired.

Oh! Must have dozed off. Ivy's giving out the
work, that's good, always liked something to do,
never idle, keeps you going, idle hands make
idle work, get down to it, I can do this, fancy
goods again, it's hard for me with my fingers but
I can do it if I set myself to it, yes, where's
the glue, ah. Roll it round nice and smooth, hold
it tight, snip it off, glue, glue, loverly glue,
and bob's your uncle!
Oh, I can do these. I'll beat Ivy today, I'll do
more than she can, if she lets me have enough
paper. Roll it round, nice and smooth, hold it
tight, snip snip and it's off, paste the glue along
the edge, press together, another one done.
Roll it round, nice and nice, hold it tight, snip it
off, off it comes, good paper this, this time,
press the glue, too much that time, never mind eh,
it's not as though she's paying us, eh, snip snip
go the scissors, I can do this without thinking, easy,

got it off to a fine art, like I used to when
I was at Fuller's, packing, we used to have
races amongst ourselves to see who could fill
most cartons first, I'd usually win, there was
only one girl who could give me a run for my
money, not that we ever bet on it, her name
was   Fair
hair, rosy cheeks she had, a bit cheeky with
the men from Bakery she was, too, given half
a chance, what was her name?

One afternoon I remember it was so hot that she
undressed right there, took everything off under
her overall and sat there in just her overall,
bold as a knocker, any of the Bakery men could
have come in just then and seen her stark naked,
we were all holding our breath at the nerve of it,
there she was, right in – *Yes, dear, what do you*
want?
Yes, I'll join you, if I can do the rolling again
like I did before. Yesterday, was it yesterday?
Forget, there must have been one day I was
beating Ivy and she kept on keeping the paper
from me so that I wouldn't beat her, but Ivy
seems to think it was yesterday we worked together,
perhaps it was, her memory may be better than mine,
mine is getting shocking.

            Yes, someone has to do the organising.
And it always seems to be you. If it's not House

Mother it's Ivy.   She's welcome.
Roll it round now, nice and easy, that's the way,
smoothly does it.   There.
              Easy.

              the still-room next to the carved
room   would wait on my own and listen
the company   lords and ladies
              sometimes   the carving
I did not like, it was heavy and dark, it did not
reach to the ceiling because it had belonged to
the older house, over the doors it said 1636 in a
shield, but the house itself was more modern, the
rooms were taller and bigger, the carving was
patterns and crests and shields of families they
were related to, or wanted it thought that they
were related to, the way
              mirrors opposite the back lawn with
a sundial
The house itself I loved from the first moment I
saw it, though it meant servitude to me, it was
the people who made me a servant
walking from the village with Megan Williams along
the galloping drive, miles of rhododendrons,
suddenly you could see a top corner of the house,
black-and-white, but big, bigger than any other
black-and-white I'd seen, though when you were
nearer you could see it wasn't wood, it was a black-
and-white pattern in plaster or something like
that   but it was a lovely house, I forgave

it that   cheating.

          the hall   Hall
     the portrait of Miss Eirwen   and the
tiny   the panelling was oak, it took
some polishing   and a great brassbound
trunk, with studs   it broke my heart
          that place died in 1939, died,
they told me

Even took away my name, didn't like Sioned,
wouldn't call me that, or even Janet, gave me
a new name to suit them, Emma, that I hated
most of all, I think.

Alyn Llywelyn said fuckit in bead-threading. I
did not know what it meant then. I don't think
he did, either. Miss Jones made a fuss about it,
she washed out his mouth with soap and water. We
did not understand, but he was careful what he said
after that. In fact, from that day on he was never
a great talker, was Alyn Llywelyn.

          Bowen gowen. *Yes, Ivy, you made a*
rhyme. No one's ever made up a rhyme about my name

before, never. Yes, we are doing well. I'll
have to catch up or I won't beat her.

      Mr David worked in the Small Library.
I would take coffee to him, with biscuits on a
tray   from the still-room   or the
kitchen   He would speak to
me in Welsh, which I did not usually use among
the other servants.   His wife had
died before I came to the Hall, he had spent
much of his time at his sisters' place since then.
               He would be working at
the Welsh books   the Small Library
was a cosy place
       sometimes he liked to talk to me,
made me feel proud of being Welsh
            the other servants were all
trying to ape being English, there was very little
Welsh spoken in the kitchen
The Factor hated to hear Welsh spoken, he swore
and bullied us if he heard us.

May we receive   that which for
grateful   until ever   after
         no one came
    was to be successful

in the fullness, the first place

The Lyons over Hammersmith station. Would go
there for tea in the war, no meal could cost
more than five shillings. Essential warwork,
indeed! Better than the British Restaurants
or the canteen at Fuller's. But even in the war,
Fuller's gave you your wedding cake if you were
getting married, free. Told him that, but he
said he wasn't going to get tied down just for
the sake of an unrationed wedding cake. We're
happy as we are, he said, Aren't we?

What's he want now,
filthy old man always fingering his backside.
Glue?   *Yes, here.*   *And have
Ivy's, too, then you won't have to stretch over
and hurt yourself so much.*   *All right
now?*   Have to be.

How many of these does she want us to do?
on and on   Still, Ivy'll
tell me when she thinks it's enough, Ivy's doing
the organising here

Finish at last
I'll say we've done a good session. Worked my
poor old fingers into an ache. Glad that's
over for one day. It makes a difference.

I've worked harder than Ron, I'm four or five
ahead of him, spare, all those. I'm good. *Yes,
here's my bits and pieces, Ivy, and good riddance!*

*Yes, pack them neatly in, crackers
for Christmas.*
Why can't we have some different coloured paper?
I'm fed up with this sort of red, rotten red.

I may not be very   but I am

Here she comes. I hope she'll like what we've done.

Ron is stupid. *They're not
bad, are they, Miss?*
Better than hers, anyway –
Oooh – she hasn't done any, Mrs Ridge!   How
does she get away with it?

So tired now. I'll drop off
in my chair soon if she doesn't watch out.

Pass the Parcel.
Haven't played that since I was a child. Sweets it
was usually, very small packet of sweets wrapped
round and round and round with lots and lots and
lots of paper and string and brown sticky paper.
It was such a let-down in the end, but that made
it all the more fun and it meant that all those
who didn't win were less disappointed when it
turned out to be next to nothing.

Oh, it's my turn.
Parcel feels exciting. On to George.
Marvellous, he moves. Passed it to Sarah, as well!
He must be getting better, old George. You never
know, he might even say something next. That would
be a miracle!

She shouldn't keep it, you can't trust that Mrs Ridge
to be fair in the slightest.   Oh, the
music's stopped, and Ron's the one to open it. I
wonder what it can be?
Eh? Not very nice at all! Why did she do that?
Poor old Ron, I feel sorry for him, his backside in
that sort of state, too. It's not right at all.

The Factor was a swine,
a swine. And he was a villain, too. He came
there with hardly a penny to his name, and died
worth twenty thousand. How he got it is a long
story. He would tell the sisters things had been
done on the estate when he knew very well they
hadn't. And he'd pocket the money, of course.
One day Miss Mary called me in to her in the great
drawing room and asked me if I knew where the Factor
was. He's gone to Birmingham, I said. To pay
the coal bill, she said, but he could have done it
by post, I gave him a cheque. I think she knew
then he was taking a backhander and had gone to
collect it. She would never hear a word against
him until then, that day I think she realised what
a villain he was, but it was too late, she was –
Travel, no, what she means by that is

Don't mind, passes the time.

But who's going to push me?

Yes, that
would be good of you, Charlie. A gentle turn
round the hall. Sure you really feel up to
it, though?

When the Factor retired, he made a bonfire of
papers from his office and it burned for three
days. He built his own house, how he ever did
that I'll never know, out of their money. How
could a man on his salary ever save twenty thousand? The family knew, of course, and tried to
tell Auntie Mary, but she would hear no word
against him. He even had his own electricity line
from the big house, a mile across the fields,
so he got his light free. Though he did good work,
I'll agree, but he never did it unless there was
a backhander in it for him. But you could never
prove anything against him, that was the difficulty.
And he had the power of life and death over some of
us, by dismissing us. Not that I ever wished to
prove anything against him, I got on quite well
with him apart – *Not at all, Charlie, not at all.*

It must have been some time after I came across
his only cousin in Rhyl, near the front, she
looked well and was well off. She would be, of
course.

We're the last to be exercising. All
the others have given up – Tourney, oh yes, I
won that last time, beat old Ron hollow, though
he does have his troubles down there. *Hang on a
minute, Charlie.* Lift, adjust, myself.
　　　That's it, over to the corner by the cupboard. *Yes.*　　　　　　　*Yes, Charlie, I can.*

Here's my mop. *What's she soaked it in this time?
Smells like what you were mixing, Charlie.*

　　　　　　　Lark is right, Charlie.
Let's get hold of this mop properly. Now where shall
I try to land it first?　　　　　　　*Off!*
　　　　　He's a good pusher, Charlie.
George's let his mop fall, get him right in the PUSS!
　　　One to me, very pleased.
　　　　　　　　Off we
go again. I shall win again, I know. George is hope-
less. Aim at chest this time, oh flinch! SHOULDER!
Still a solid blow, his hardly flicked me with wet.
Good, eh?
　　　Last time. I'll aim for his breadbasket
this go.　　　Carefully, carefully.
　　　　　GOT HIM!
　　　　　Mrs Bowen the Champion, she
should have said. Twice I've won now, I'm the Champion,

I've never won many things in my life, but I'm
the Champion here.

There   it comes over me
            again
                                    faintness

                                            won't last
long

            not long

                                    It just takes
some   time   before   you're
back to yourself   again.

Auntie Mary did leave me something in her will.
They were good like that, remembering. It was very
little. They didn't used to give pensions to their
staff however long they'd been there, they left a
lump sum in their will, the sisters.   Fat
comfort to some.
A little use to me now, I can buy myself the odd
Guinness if I can find anyone to go out for it for
me.   They had their own
bread, we baked every other day. But no brewer,

though, they were teetotal, very strict. Not Chapel,
church, but very teetee just the same. They
knew the gardeners drank ale with their dinners,
but woe betide anyone who brought it into the
Hall!   I did once, felt ever
so guilty. I was low at the time and I bought
myself a small bottle of gin from the Bear. Normally I felt so safe in my little attic room, well,
it was not so little, it was a reasonable size,
but all the time I had that bottle in the room I
felt as though I were a criminal.   My little
room. The washstand with the plain green jug
and bowl, the window, quite big really, looking
down on the lawns and across the bridge to the
warren. I had some happy hours there, it was not
all hardship. Most of the time I didn't have to
share it, only if we had Company and they had
servants.   My bed
along one side, and an old easy chair, the high-
backed sort with wings, donkeys' years old, a
picture Miss Eirwen had painted herself, brown
lino on the floor. I was content – no, at the
time I hated every minute of being a servant,
only now does it seem
                        pleasant.
                        The lilac
curtains, my own flowery jerry under the bed,
but clothes behind the curtains in the alcove.
They may be like it still, the Hall is still there,
I should think, but now it is probably a guesthouse

or something like that, perhaps they've sold it to
build houses on, chopped down all those lovely
trees.   Everything changes,
nothing gets better.

                           I was going
to read myself, but daren't now she's given Ivy
a taste of her tongue.   But I'm
not going to watch this filth again, why she does
it baffles me. Surely she can't think it stirs
us up?

                   Summer we would go down the
bothy, where the single gardeners lived, next to
the walled garden and the greenhouses. They'd grow
all sorts for the sisters there, figs and peaches
you didn't get anywhere else in the county, or so
they said.   A boilerhouse
in the basement of the bothy, coal down a chute,
the long winters. I can remember it exactly, why
can't I remember what happened yesterday?

                My friends would say I was forward,
just because I used to look men right in the eyes.
None of that shy retiring for me. That's what men
and women's eyes are for, I would say to them.
They knew what I meant, they would giggle.
                 Rabbits were common, we
had trout out of the stream, too, poached, the
sisters did not make a fuss about that sort of
thieving like some of the gentry around those parts.
Why trout were thought so special I could never

understand, anyone who'd had them as often as I have would prefer a good fresh herring any day.

      Listen to her!

                  No, doesn't matter

age	89
marital status	bachelor
sight	10%
hearing	15%
touch	25%
taste	20%
smell	10%
movement	15%
CQ count	2
pathology	contractures; incontinent; advanced inanition; chronic rheumatoid arthritis; Paget's Disease; advanced senile depression; muscle atrophy; fibrositis; intermittent renal failure; among many others.

Lame

source

unfr

they'll

for

why?

oughter

eh!

schools

consuls

how are you? in the

pink

straining

Cox's Orange   pippin!

No matter if the future's dim
keep right on and suffer hymn

Work!   work   Fancy, aaah

crêpe paper, crêper   crêpep   crêper

crêp

crêper

crêper?

crêper!

crêper, yes

Stick   she says? *Eh?*
                         crêper
     glue   little round
                         Sweeties are they?

glass

spitting spitting spitting

maybe, ah

Thorban, thorban

seal

floors

with

full

continued

of, of, of

some

gilli

grim

at

point of

in

does

there are

in does

in does

will

sake

best

my

my

hoarse

which

to

                              still

                                             my
name   Eh!   anger at me,
she   no more!   no more meat and gravy
and?   oh.   it's   oh dear, what have I
been doing?   she goes
              there
                        there

a mess, *yes*.   but she's not   no
                 fear

        cheek

when I get better

Package

for me   pass, parc

what?

quite

three and six nine and six fifteen

                           name   it

               moving   moving!

everything's moving!

                       ?

moving

                      stopped   good

           what's this?

                                jerk

        moving   this

stick

                                oooooooooh!

splashash   what was?   smell

     mop   not   this   mop

          what?

                               aaaagh!

    shoulder!

                   blank

    aaaaaaaaagh!

No, doesn't matter

age	94
marital status	not known
sight	5%
hearing	10%?
touch	5%
taste	15%
smell	20%
movement	5%
CQ count	o
pathology	everything everyone else has; plus incipient bronchial pneumonia; atherosclerotic dementia; probably ament; hemiplegia (with negative Babinski response); to name only a very few.

Galluog

lwcus

ynad

noddwr

Teg

enwog

geirwir

arabus

iachus

Hael

uchaf

grymus

hwyliog

eofn   sylfaen

Math

addien

reit

gorwych

anianol

rhyw

ethol

ter

Huawdl

uchelryw

graslawn

hoyw

eirian

serennu

Afal

llu

uned

nesaf

Teilwng

egniol

gris

arlun

ieuanc

Hogyn

uthr

gogoniant

huan

epil

syber!

Disglair

addurno

fyny

ynni

digrif

drud

Tirion

eisen

gwron

atodiad

ifanc

      Hadu

unol

                       golenad

   haul

        eryr

          safon

                    I am

t e r r i b l e, I v y

      N o w I c a n   e v e r y
w o r d y o u s a y   I am a prisoner in my
self. It is terrible. The movement agonises me.

Let me out, or I shall die

                   No, I do
n o t g e t   a n y
l i g h t e r, I v y,
           I   i n -
     t   e   n   d
            n   o   t
t   o   g   e   t
          a   n   y -
t   h   i   n   g
        a   n   y
m   o   r   e

           n   o

m   o   r

age	42
marital status	divorcée
sight	85%
hearing	90%
touch	100%
taste	40%
smell	95%
movement	100%
CQ count	10
pathology	mild clap; incipient influenza; dandruff; malignant cerebral carcinoma (dormant).

They are fed, they are my friends. Is that not enough?
And what would be enough?   Some of them indeed are not
capable of differentiating between meat and bread – no, that
is not an argument for not giving them meat. A balanced
diet is essential to the health of the aged. I know that.
I know what is best for them. I am a trained House Mother.
Did I not work under Frau Holstein of the House in Basle?
Ah! Sunny days sitting on the slopes of the Moron, or walking
by the green river, with that good, good, woman.
Yes, I know what I am talking about, friend, as regards
diet and everything else to do with the efficient running of
a tidy. . . . . *No! You can't have any more meat, you gutsy greedy
old slobbery cow!* The impertinence of it! And what does she
think of next? I can read her like a book – she is after Ron's
meat, a birdlike eater, Ron, the twitcher will stop her. *No!
Three from the twitcher for thieves, Mrs Ridge, one! two! three!*

There! That will teach you, Mrs Ridge!
Treat them like children: they are children, aren't they?
        This is truly their second childhood, isn't it?
           Oh, do not think I justify
myself! I have no psychological need to do that, friend, none
at all. Do not deceive yourself: deception is a sin if not a
crime.

*Now come on, finish up like good second children. There's
all the treats of our weekly Social Evening to come.*

        So many of them look beautiful,
manage to keep some beauty, even acquire some beauty. I use
the word advisedly. Even the bearded Stanton lady, in her
way.   *Come along now!* Chivvy chivvy chivvy. Daydreaming, most of them, they remember years ago far better
than they remember to change themselves, or ask to be
changed. They admire the past, think so much of the past: why
therefore do they expect treatment any different from that
they would have received in the workhouse of the past?
Ah, you can bet, friend, they prefer at least this aspect of
modern life, do not want to return to the good old workhouse
days!   Oh dear me, no, no!
    Isn't that a not unpleasing paradox?
           This may be a
charitable institution, that may be the form of words, but
it is as remote from what was known as a workhouse as my
Ralphie is from a

    dingo.

Right now! Clear up!   *Quietly,*
if you please, this is not a bandhouse or bothy! What d'you
imagine you're at?   *Quietly!*

                              At least we
don't have washing up to do with these cardboard plates.
Just shoot the lot for pigswill, sell it. Must see if I
can get more off that swine Berry, ha, though he gets
enough off me one way or the other, besides the odd
bit of the other. I give him a good class of swill for
his pigs, they must enjoy the cardboard, I think. Pigs
eat anything, they say. No complaints, anyway, and it's
all good for – *You dirty old . . . person!*
                    What a mess, dropped the lot!
Thought you were feeding Ralphie, did you? I tell you
Ralphie wouldn't touch it after you had!   *He*
has only the finest dogmeat, two tins a day, two large
tins, that is.   *Come here, Ralphie my darling, did*
they try to tempt you with muck, Ralphie?
                    There, there.   Feel the flowing of
those muscles, how tense he strains.   Five
times!   What a dog!
                    Mrs Bowen, I think we'll make that
your last chance to drop anything, shall we?
Come on now!   Last one to clear up is a cissy!   Really
must get on to the office again about help. Can't run
this place any longer with just a part-time cook. And
I'm not cooking once more in that place when she's off
sick or drunk. They'll have to give me help, have to.

          Right, at last
we've finished clearing up our mess, haven't we, and
so now it's time for the House Song.   *Not*
to say the House Hymn!

                  Are we ready,
then?   *Altogether now, let's be hearing*
from you in the Balcony as well, one,
                two,
                    three!

     The joys of life continue strong
     Throughout old age, however long:
     If only you can cheerful stay
     And brightly welcome every day.
     Not what you've been, not what you'll be,
     What matters now is that you're free:
     The joys of life continue strong
     Throughout old age, however long.

     The most important thing to do
     Is stay alive and screw and screw:
     No matter if the future's dim
     So long as I can use my quim:
     For I know best, and bring no cheer,
     Oh, lucky me, that I am here!
     The most important thing to do
     Is screw and screw, and screw and screw.

                What a delightful song that is!

Now it's work, everyone, work, and then play, play
later. Our little good deed for the day, work.

                                        Ivy,
fetch the boxes, please.   It's Fancy Goods
again tonight, my dears, Fancy Goods except for
Sarah and Charlie who I've got something very special
in mind for.   Now my little Fancy Goods man
wasn't too pleased with the work you did yesterday,
I'm sorry to say – sorry for your sakes, that is, not
for mine, of course. Can we just be a little
bit more careful tonight?   Not get the
sticky glue all over our fingers but only where it's
supposed to go?   Ivy, give me one of those here.

            You see, it's quite simple: you
just cut your crêpe paper to the width of your little
wooden roller,   roll
it round   like this   and very carefully
glue all along the edge – very carefully, mind you,
very carefully.   You don't need
much glue, just a smear, just a smear along one edge.
                Is that all clear?
So do let's do our little good deed for the day, but
do it well if we're going to do it at all.   Ivy,
give out the work then, please.

            Sarah and Charlie,
my trusties, I have something special for you tonight.

*Charlie, I want you to pour about
a quarter of each of these bottles into one of the
empty ones here until it's three-quarters full –
three bottles pour a quarter out of, that is, until
this one's also three-quarters full, and when you've
got them all three-quarters full then top them up
with water from your tap.   All right?
But please be careful not to stain any of the labels
with drips, there's a good trusty, my old Charlie?*

*No, I know you haven't, I
know, Charlie.   Now Sarah, I want
you to do a similar job for me, though not quite the
same. You see these little bottles? I'd like you
just to soak the labels off, make the bottles quite
clean afterwards.
        No, I don't want the labels kept for
anything, no, so you can get them off any way you
like, tear them, scrape them with your nails, oh?
                Yes, by all means
use a knife from the washing up.*

*Everyone happy, then?   Ivy, see that everyone
has a pot of glue and enough to get on with.
        All right, friends?
        I'm going to work, too, get on with my own
work up on the stage.*

*Talk by all means, but let's not have too much
noise, eh?   Bless you.*

My children. From this dais
I am monarch of all I survey. This is my Empire.
I do not exaggerate, friend. They are dependent
upon me and upon such minions as I have from time
to time. Nothing is more sure than that I am
in control of them. And they know it. They
vie with each other for my attention. This is
especially noticeable on the tablet round
each night and morning. On the weekly medical
round their attention is divided between the
good doctor and myself: they are undecided as
to whether to play for the once-a-week prestige
of his attention, or for mine that it may
perhaps be available more than once a week,
perhaps even daily. Oh, how comic that is!
For I love only Ralphie, Ralphie is my darling!
Where are you, Ralphie?
Ralph, come here at once!   The dirty doggie,
licking at that mess under poor old Mrs Stanton!
Hope it's only water. Perhaps it's gravy from
dinner. There, there, Ralphie, there's a good
dog, that's my hairy darling.

There are always complaints, of course. Complaining
is one of the few activities into which they put
some genuine feeling. It is good for them, of course.
I listen very carefully to their complaints. And then
do nothing. There is nothing for them really to
complain about here. They would be so much worse off
if they were not in here. The hazards of hypothermia,

falls, neglect. But it does not worry me if
complaining is their favourite occupation. It is
also a way of vieing for my attention. I fondle
Ralphie in front of them and that keeps up their
interest. It frustrates them and gives them a
reason to be going on. What would become of them
if I took this away? Oh, I did not study for five
years for nothing, friend, or waste my time as an
abject disciple of Frau Holstein, no! It gives them
something to worry about instead of worrying
about their reactions not being as sharp as they
were, their voices not quite so resonant, that
they are forgetful, and confused, and so on and
so forth. And then there are the diversions I
provide, as well. The Sally Army comes round
collecting several times a month. They enjoy
that, it is one of their favourite treats. Come
and join. Then we have the Olde Tyme Evening
provided by the Council once a year, too, when
they're not too busy. Oh, to them it must seem
like one mad merry-go-round! And a schoolchildren's
choir every now and again. Then there's always
the telly, when it's working – that reminds me,
must get it repaired again: it's over two months,
now. In return, they do these little jobbies for
me. Handicrafts, felt toys last month. And now
Christmas crackers, in due season.
They seem to be getting on reasonably well. Of
course, I can't expect Mrs Stanton and George to
do very much. But the important thing for them is

that it is there in front of them to be done if they
do wake up or otherwise become capable of doing
it. That really is the important thing, we all agree.
All the books agree.   I give
Mrs Stanton about three weeks, and George could
pop off any minute.
But I must get down to my work, too. *Here, Ralphie!*
                           Come and lie comfortingly on
my feet while I work on my accounts.

Have to be careful with these, no names, no initials
either, or at least not the right ones.

                           Frederick, first names will do. Do I
need to keep accounts? Yes, for my own benefit.
Frederick, then, 350 boxes filled with felt toy bits,
how much, at fivepence a box, five hundred pence a
hundred boxes, a fiver a hundred boxes, three-and-a-
half fivers are seventeen pounds and a half, fifty
pence.   So.   That he still
owes me. When will he be round with another lot?
Can't tell. It's that sort of business. He must be
on some big purchase tax fiddle. Income tax, too,
I shouldn't wonder.
Then there was the penicillin. Lump sum for
altering that lot. Twenty pounds. Shipped abroad,
no doubt, as something or other that it isn't. But
that's none of my business, it doesn't worry me,
either. My job is to keep my friends happy, and,
if it makes money, then so much the better. Do

you not agree, friend? Oh, again, do not think
I have to justify myself!
Seventeen plastic ashtrays: one pound exactly,
a job lot.   Contacts are all-important
in this business. It is not enough just to ad-
vertise in the trade papers. I must write to a
number, a large number, of likely sources of
employment. I must point out to them the unique
advantages of my methods of outworking. This
should – Ah, Charlie, my old trusty, I can tell
when you have that lost look on your face that
you are not puzzling over some problem of
philosophy, or even of filling those bottles, but
merely and genteelly trying to fart without Sarah
or anyone else noticing. Charlie.
                    Ralphie warm on my feet.

        What you do not understand, I think,
friend, is that what we imagine they want for themselves is not actually what they do want. I do
not know what they want, either. But I do know
that they are certainly not as we are, and that
therefore by definition they do not want what we
want.   How does anyone know
what anyone else really wants?   Multiply
that by the diffusing effect of time, friend,
which alters with every day, every minute,
virtually! When I was eight I wanted to be a fairy
in a ballet, ho ho ho! he he he! ha ha ha! heh!
heh! heh! and similar printers' straitjackets for

the gusty, exploding liberation of laughter.
But I forget myself.   Where was I?
Yes, the Divisional Officer asked me whether I
would like to undertake a week's exchange with
a seaside House. Really, I said to him, don't
you think that would be rather absurd with my
group of friends? Besides (though I didn't tell
him this) I had my Stationery Goods quota to
meet that week. Which reminds me: how many
sets of pens and rulers was it he still owes
me for? Look it up.

        Yes, 230. I'll have to mention that to
him when he comes, whenever. Can't be too careful. That shows the value of keeping accounts.
It's certain he wouldn't have remembered it, con-
veniently, unless I'd mentioned it.

Don't think I do this for the money, friend. The
Council takes all their pensions and allows them
back one pound each for their personal expenditure.
That is too much, to my way of thinking. They have
no need of that much pocket money. No, friend,
not for their money: you can see there is little
chance here of the quick oncer.

Ah, Charlie has nearly finished. He'll be asking
me about corks soon.   I'll go down now.
The rest might as well finish now, too.

*Right now, everyone. You can finish now. You've
done a good session of work, and so now you
deserve to play.* But let's clear up first,
shall we? *Ivy, please collect the boxes for
us.* Descend from my throne.

Charlie, yes, I knew you'd ask. *You've got corks
from the ones which were full, haven't you?*
Good. *Then here's
some more for the others. Just stand the boxes
in the corner if you will, please, afterwards.*

*Ralphie! Come away from that! You all right,
Mrs Stanton?* Right as she'll ever be. Done no
work at all. *George, you've just been
daydreaming!* And screwing up the bits of
paper and getting the bleeding glue all over the
place! Ugh! Still, what
did I expect?
*How about you, Mrs Bowen? You've been working
with Ivy and Ron, have you? Very nicely, too.
You've done a lot between you.* Yes, yes.
*And greedy old Mrs Ridge,
you haven't done any!* *Don't you cheek
me or you'll get another taste of the twitcher, the
twitcher!* *Now then!*

*Very good, Sarah, my old trusty, what a lovely job
you've made of those!* *I'm very pleased with you,
very pleased indeed.* *Yes, and you, Charlie.*

Now let's have some relaxation. Attention please,
everyone! 　　　　　　　　*Stay where you are,*
sitting round the long table, and we're going to
play Pass the Parcel. You pass the parcel from
one to another, and when the music stops whoever
has it tries to open it. When the music starts
again, the parcel must be passed on. And so on.
And what a lovely surprise the last one's going to
get, the winner! Here we go then. You start off
with the music, Sarah. 　　　　　*Off we go!*
Music on.

　　　　　　　　　　　　　　　Stop
at Mrs Ridge.

On again.

　　　　　　　Music stopped at Sarah. Give her
a treat, she's worked well, give her a bit of ex-
citement. On again.

　　　　Oh my darlings, how I love you!

Pass it on, Mrs Ridge! While the music's playing it . . .
I should think so. 　　　　　　Stop the music.
Who's won, then? Yes, it's Ron! Ron's the lucky winner!
　　　　You're right, Ron, first time. It's SHIT!
But whose shit is it? That's the question! I'll sing it
for you: 　　　*Pass the parcel, pass the parcel,*
　　　　　　　See what comes from RALPHIE'S arsehole!

How disgusting! you must be saying to yourself,
friend, and I cannot but agree. But think a bit
harder, friend: why do I disgust them?
I disgust them in order that they may not be
disgusted with themselves. I am disgusting to them
in order to objectify their disgust, to direct it to
something outside themselves, something harmless.
Some of them still believe in God: what would
happen if they were to turn their disgust on God
for taking away control over their own sphincter
muscles, for instance, and think, naturally enough,
that He must be vile to be responsible for such
a thing?   Far better for them to think
handling and smelling and seeing doggie's turd is
disgusting!   Do you not agree?
Right, everyone! Attention please! The game is
over and now it's our Travel Time.   It's so
much more tasteful an expression than Exercise,
don't you think, friend?   *Travel Time. Yes, I*
know your old bones protest, but you know it's good
for you. Those of you who can walk push round those
in wheelchairs, those in wheelchairs move everything
you can move as you go.   *Off we go now!*

There are worse conditions and worse places, friend.
I have worked in geriatric wards where the stench of
urine and masturbation was relieved only by the odd
gangrenous limb or advanced carcinoma. Where confused
patients ate each other's puke. Where I have seen a
nurse spray a patient's privates with an aerosol

lavatory deodorant. Even worse, people like
these can be put away in mental wards and homes
when they are perfectly sane, simply because they
are old: they don't stay perfectly sane long.
They are stripped of their spectacles, false teeth,
everything personal to them. They are shut away,
visits are rare and discouraged anyway, no one cares;
they are forgotten and wholly in the power of nurses
who have been known to make them alter their wills,
to scatter the ward's pills for everyone to scramble
for, and to put Largactil in the tea unmeasured.
This is a happy House, friend, a holiday camp,
compared. Here I give them constant occupation, and,
most important, a framework within which to establish
– indeed, to possess – their own special personalities.
Here we respect their petty possessions, so important
to them but rubbish to us.
This is the time when the bearing surfaces of the
joints begin to wear seriously, when the walls of the
veins and arteries harden, when the nervous system
loses much of its subtlety. It has always been so.
Today we can give them more time, by nylon balls and
sockets, drugs to thin the blood, Largactil to lift
nervous depression: but ultimately these are nothing.
                         You should understand the
simple fact that they are all approaching death very
quickly; and one must help them to do so in the right
spirit. It is what used to be called a holy duty. I
did not invent this system: I inherited it. And in
the end death will come to me too, probably.

There. They enjoy it. Sometimes for a change I
have them doing Travel in the form of bizarre sexual
antics. As-if-sexual, that is, in the case of some
friends.   And now I give you – *SPORT!*
Yes, it's Tourney Time again, friends! Remember how
you enjoyed the last Tourney we had?
Of course you do! Get the wet mops, Ivy, please. And
Charlie, you wheel Mrs Bowen to one corner, and
you, Sarah, wheel George to the opposite corner.
                        That's it. One mop each,
Ivy, thank you.
On the word, then, steeds and knights, you thunder
at top speed towards each other, never flinching,
like bold and parfait gentil knights, and try to
lance each other. No stopping! Straight on, turn,
and back for another joust. Ready then? And may the
best knight win!   One!   Two!   Three!

            Well done, Mrs Bowen! A palpable hit!
One more time, then.   Off you go!

Another hit for Mrs Bowen! Sarah, see if George is
still awake, will you? He doesn't seem to be trying
very hard.   Last joust, then. Away you go!
                    At various times in the past we
have had Balloon Races, Polo, Folk Dancing and Archery.
Mrs Bowen the Winner! Back to the table, now. The
Knobbly Knee Competition was very popular, too.

*So after all our exertions let's just have a quiet
discussion session, shall we? And as always our
subject is* HOW I WANT TO GO *and its related topics* MY CHOICE
OF COFFIN *or* WHAT I WANT DONE WITH MY EARTHLY
REMAINS. *First of all, let us remember first principles.
Death may be seen as the price paid for what the body
is – that is, the very biological functioning of
the body, its very nature, inherently implies and
contains death; this debt is paid in instalments;
and the period of old age is that in which all
arrears must be settled. Death indeed may often be a lot
less painful than life: the actual dying, that is.
There are various ways of facing this death. Whether you
believe in God or not, there is still the possibility
he or she will be there waiting for you after death: those
of you wishing for a coin to be placed in your mouths or
victuals to be provided for a postulated journey have only
to let us know. Again, you may see death as the exchange of individual life for biological improvement
and conservation as part of a scheme for higher ful-
filment on the part of some life force. Or you can
simply see yourselves as potentially a heap of rather
superior manure: there is, in fact, no dishonour in
that. However you look at it, someone has to decide what
to do with what you leave behind you, and as this is a
democratic institution we give you this opportunity to
decide, for yourselves, between burial, cremation, acid
bath, remote moorland exposure, or whatever.*

     No replies. Never are.   I just hand them over to an
undertaker who probably uses them for meat pies, anyway.

And now at last what you have all been waiting for:
Entertainment! Up on the stage for this, so that
they can see better.
Here's one you'll all enjoy. A little girl, let's
call her Dottie, was sitting on her grandad's knee
and said: "Grandad, were you in the Ark?" "No, of
course I wasn't!" said the Grandad, somewhat taken
aback. "Then why," said delightful little Dottie,
"weren't you drownded?" Isn't
that a funny one? Laugh, you stupid old twats!
Here's another one, even better.
Most of you are at the metallic stage of your lives:
silver in your hair, gold in your teeth, and, in the
case of the men, lead in your trousers!
Laugh!
I'll give them just one more. *There was a*
very old couple. The husband was ninety-eight and
the wife was ninety-five. One day their son died,
aged seventy-two. The husband consoled his grief-
stricken wife by saying: "There, there, dear, we never
did think we'd live to see him grow up."
All right, so it's
a rotten joke. What do you expect, professional comics?

But I must just tell you this last one. A man lying
on his deathbed was asked if he had made his peace
with God. "I didn't know we had ever had a row,"
said the man, wittily.
Isn't that screamingly funny?
Mind you, he didn't get into heaven either.

A slight laugh. How curious that
heaven does concern some of them in the way – *Ivy!*
How dare you read a book during Entertainment! Who
do you think you are? How dare you?
                        I should think so too! You'd
all better watch now, it's the Piece de Resistance.
            Turn on the sexy music.   *Ralphie!*
Here, boy.   Here we go, then, sway, that's
it, just right, slowly unbutton my overall, so they
can see I have only a bra
then only tights   underneath
                    cast off the overall over Ralphie. Up
on the table   slowly down with my stocking
tights   one leg   the other   *I can*
see you're enjoying this!   All watching, except
Mrs Stanton, asleep or dead – does it matter? Now
my bra, tantalise by appearing to have difficulty.
                    Wouldn't they all rather be dead?
Ah, friend, that is where we make a mistake! For
they would all rather be alive! All!   Tights,
gossamer, off   stand! And the music swells to
an early climax.   *Here, Ralphie! Up on the table*
with Mummy!   That's it, you know what to do with
your long probing red Borzoi tongue, don't you, Ralphie!
                            Lovely!
            oooooh!
                        that's it!
        Oh, Ralphie! Faster! we're getting near the
end of the page, Ralphie!   oooooh!   oh!
iiiiiihl!   oooooh!   nearly!   *YES!*

        There! Wasn't that wonderful!
I know you too have your little feels in the
toilets. Good luck to you! I hope you enjoy
them as much as I do.   And now we must be
in just the mood to sing the Jubilate before we
all vanish up our own orifices.
All together now!   One   Two   Three!

            Death comes to all, no matter who,
            No matter what we bloody do:
            Despite lacrosse, P.E. and gym,
            Our lights at last will surely dim.
            For this we should stand up and cheer
            And please ourselves while we are here:
            Death comes to all, no matter who,
            No matter what you bloody do!

And here you see, friend, I am about to step

outside the convention, the framework of twenty-
one pages per person. Thus you see I too am the
puppet or concoction of a writer (you always knew
there was a writer behind it all? Ah, there's
no fooling you readers!), a writer who has me at
present standing in the post-orgasmic nude but
who still expects me to be his words without
embarrassment or personal comfort.   So
you see this is from his skull. It is a diagram
of certain aspects of the inside of his skull!
                    What a laugh!

Still, I'll finish off for him, about the sadness,
the need to go farther better to appreciate the
nearer, what you have now: if you are not like
our friends, friend, laugh now, prepare, accept,
worse times are a-coming, nothing is more sure.

But here's something he found in the Montgomeryshire
Collections and thought you might like to have
for yourself, friend:

> F for Francis
> I for Chances
> N for Nicholas
> I for Tickle us
> S for Sammy the
>   Salt Box